Sunny.

Sunny.♥

Stacey Pyne

Sunny
Published by Stacey Pyne
with Castle Publishing
New Zealand
Instagram: goldie_the_book
www.goldiethebook.com

ISBN 978-0-473-58139-8 (Softcover)
ISBN 978-0-473-58140-4 (ePUB)
ISBN 978-0-473-58141-1 (Kindle)

Editing:
Iola Goulton & Andrea Candy

Illustration:
Milla Pyne

Production & Typesetting:
Andrew Killick
Castle Publishing Services
www.castlepublishing.co.nz

Cover Design:
Stephen Kirkby
hi@parkbyprojects.com

For Leith and Donna Thompson
(Mum and Dad)

Prologue

'What should I do? How will I help?' she asked him.
   'Just keep writing,' he replied.
   And so she did.

Publish his glorious deeds among the nations. Tell every-one about the amazing things he does. (Psalm 96:3)

Traits

There are certain traits that belong to men, some learned and others natural.

Whenever Eliud coughed, he would hold one hand over his mouth and pat his chest with the other. This was a learned trait—his mother had watched Eliud's father, Akim, do the same thing. Now that her son was grown with children of his own, she saw her husband in him each time he coughed. Eleazer picked up this same trait from his father Eliud, who then passed it down through Matthan to Jacob and onto Joseph.

Jesus sat before the crowd, the sun beating down on his head. He paused between sentences and took a deep breath before continuing. Dust was drawn into his throat from the path beside them as more people joined those gathered. As Jesus coughed, he held one hand over his mouth and patted his chest with the other.

Akim was the father of Eliud. Eliud was the father of Eleazar. Eleazar was the father of Matthan. Matthan was the father of Jacob. Jacob was the father of Joseph, the husband of Mary. Mary gave birth to Jesus, who is called the Messiah. (Matthew 1:14–16)

You feel like wide open spaces.
When I come to you, there is room to breathe here.

He lets me rest in green meadows;
he leads me beside peaceful streams.
(Psalm 23:2)

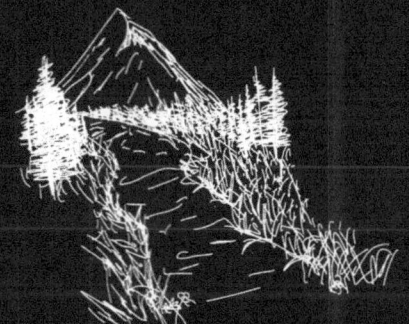

Persy

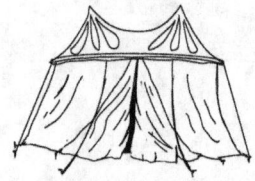

Persy was an Israelite boy from the tribe of Levi. He lived in a tent with his mother and father and two younger sisters. Persy lived a simple life close to God's holy sanctuary. As a Levite, Persy and his family and their tribe were responsible for taking care of God's home. Persy felt special, knowing that of all the tribes, the Levites were the only people allowed to come close to God's home.

He had grown to understand why—because the Levite tribe belonged to God, as a replacement for all the firstborn sons of Israel. Persy did not belong to himself, but to God. He smiled to himself at the thought. Persy was pleased he belonged to God. Whenever the Israelite community packed up camp to move somewhere else, Persy's father would let Persy help him with his sacred work. Persy's father was responsible for the lampstand that stood beside the Ark. It was a special responsibility, and Persy would stand silently, watching his father in awe until he called him over and assigned him a chore. Persy understood that because he belonged to God, it made sense that he and his family would care for God's sacred objects.

It was early morning, and Persy was the first to wake up. He could hear the soft breathing of his parents close by, and his sisters were quiet. Persy decided he would get up quietly and creep outside to watch the sun come up. He tiptoed across the earth floor as quietly as he could, and pulled his tent door aside, closing it behind him. He sat down close to the opening. Fires smouldered from the evening before, sending streams of smoke into the air. It was too dark to see far, but it wouldn't be long before other children popped their heads out from their tents. The children always rose first. Twenty minutes passed, and Persy played with a stone and a small stick on the ground around his crossed legs.

'Persy,' his mother whispered from inside. He swivelled on his bottom and poked his head back inside their tent.

'I'm here, Mum,' he replied.

'Come and give me a cuddle,' his Mum whispered, and Persy smiled in the dark that was slowly becoming brighter. He was eight years old now, almost too old to cuddle his Mum in her bed. But as long as no one was watching, Persy secretly still loved to. He crawled beneath her blanket. The girls woke up shortly after, and Persy's father rose too.

Persy got dressed and tidied away his bed.

'Persy, have you checked the cloud today?' Mum asked.

'No,' Persy replied. 'I forgot to check!' It was one of Persy's chores each morning to check on the cloud of the Lord which hovered above his home, the tabernacle. The cloud travelled with the Israelite community. It shone like a fire in the night and a cloud during the day. During the day, the cloud of the Lord hovered over his tabernacle and then the Israelites knew that they were to stay put, to continue to camp where they were. But if the cloud lifted from the tabernacle, the Israelites would pack up camp and follow the cloud. It was Persy's job to check whether the cloud was still hovering over the tabernacle.

Persy and his family and their community had been camping in the same location for so many months that Persy had lost count. It might even be close to a year since they had last moved. Persy strapped his second sandal on and jumped to his feet.

'I'll check now, Mum.' He pulled the tent door aside and was met by sunlight pouring into their tent. He stepped outside, tied the door up to let the sun in, and turned towards the tabernacle. His heart skipped a beat—something had changed.

The cloud had lifted.

'It's lifted,' he whispered to himself, hardly believing his eyes. He had checked the cloud for many, many mornings now, and it was always the same thing. He turned to announce the news to his family.

'Mum, Dad!' He ducked his head back into the tent, the excitement in his voice rising. 'It's lifted! The cloud has lifted!'

Whenever the cloud lifted from over the sacred tent, the people of Israel would break camp and follow it. And wherever the cloud settled, the people of Israel would set up camp. In this way, they travelled and camped at the Lord's command wherever he told them to go. Then they remained in their camp as long as the cloud stayed over the Tabernacle. Whether the cloud stayed above the Tabernacle for two days, a month, or a year, the people of Israel stayed in camp and did not move on. But as soon as it lifted, they broke camp and moved on. (Numbers 9:17–18, 22)

The Pathway

Deep beneath the waters, at the bottom of the sea, lay a hidden pathway. It stretched out before him, untouched and undisturbed on the floor of the ocean as though waiting—hidden, like treasure. The path wound this way and that with the ebb and flow of the current. It ran over the seabed, over cockleshells, and beneath ocean plants and algae, and deeper still. A path constructed by no human hands. A secret pathway, its location unknown to all of mankind. Why would he need a path on the floor of the ocean? To where would it lead? And to whom would he reveal it?

When the Red Sea saw you, O God, its waters looked and trembled! The sea quaked to its very depths.
Your road led through the sea, your pathway through the mighty waters—a pathway no one knew was there! You led your people along that road like a flock of sheep, with Moses and Aaron as their shepherds. (Psalm 77:16, 19–20)

Noah

Noah stood with her sisters before Moses and the people. She held her head high and set her face, even though her hands were trembling. Noah was determined to appear confident and unafraid. She cleared her throat. It was her role to address the leaders. When it came to her sisters, it was always her.

Noah had been outspoken since day one, something that had often landed her in trouble. When their father had been alive, he'd scolded her more times than she could count. He would try to remind Noah of her place, that she was a woman and needed to behave like one. Noah didn't like behaving like a woman. She often watched the men around her and yearned for the position they held in the Israelite society. Sometimes Noah found life as a woman boring. She didn't speak of it, not unless she was alone with Mahlah. Mahlah was more than just Noah's sister—she was her best friend. But Mahlah didn't share the same passion for having a voice as Noah. Mahlah was lovely and quiet, like all good girls should be. Although Noah was not, they had been inseparable since they were children.

A hand reached for Noah's, which she held behind her back. She knew it was Mahlah. Noah held on tight.

It had been months since their father had died after becoming sick in the wilderness. Zelo had been a good man and had been kind to Noah and her sisters, though he never had a son. When he died, the girls had been left to fend for themselves.

This was the reason they stood together now, united in their decision to make their request of Moses and the leaders.

Since their father had died and there were no sons to inherit from him, all that belonged to Zelo would no longer belong to his family. His property would not be given to Noah and her sisters, because they were female. It made Noah wild. But she took a deep breath. She would hold it together and communicate as calmly and clearly as she could. Noah knew her sisters stood behind her, praying silently. Noah squeezed Mahlah's hand before releasing it and stepping forward to address Moses, the leaders, and the people.

'Thank you for meeting us today.' Noah looked at Moses as she spoke. She would concentrate on him, because he was the one God spoke to. Moses nodded at Noah in response.

'Our father died in the wilderness.' Noah would get straight to the point. Moses had known their father, and she hoped he would hear her out and not dismiss their request as soon as he heard it. They were dividing the land up and giving portions out to all of their community—but not to Noah and her sisters.

'But he had no sons.' Noah went on.

'Our request is that you give us property, along with our relatives.' Noah spread her arms, towards her sisters standing behind her. Noah should stop there, but the words bubbled up within her and slipped out from between her lips.

'Why should the name of our father disappear from his clan just because he had no sons?'

There was a stirring in the crowd behind her, and Noah knew she had potentially gone too far with her last statement. But it was the truth as far as she was concerned. And this, no doubt, was her one and only chance to be heard. She was pleased. She held Moses's eyes for some time before nodding and stepping back into line beside her sisters.

'I will bring your case before the Lord,' Moses finally replied. With that, he turned to leave. Noah let out the breath she had been holding, relief washing over her. Mahlah gripped her hand once again.

'You did it,' she whispered, then kissed Noah on the cheek. Her sisters gathered around her, their relief evident.

'Well, that's all we can do now,' Noah said to them. 'Now we must leave it in God's hands.' The girls agreed as they made their way back to their tents, and the crowds dispersed. Noah didn't mind the attention she was getting from the other Israelites as she made her way home. She knew many would disagree with what she had said, but perhaps some would understand their predicament. Whatever they thought of her, Noah had succeeded in what she believed was right.

Noah woke early the following morning. She'd had a restless sleep, going back and forth over the words she had chosen when addressing Moses. Most of all, she'd worried about what they would do if God didn't permit them to share in their father's inheritance.

The people gathered before Moses once more. Noah and her sisters stood at the front of the crowd. He didn't keep them waiting today. In fact, it seemed as if he was in a rush as he approached the girls. Perhaps he had somewhere else he needed to be.

Noah practised slowing down her breathing to try to calm herself as she waited. So much hung on this decision.

'The Lord has spoken to me,' Moses said.

Noah stood up straight, to attention. Her pulse raced and she felt a little light-headed.

'The Lord says the claim of the daughters of Zelo is legitimate.' Somebody let out a little squeal behind Noah, and tears filled Noah's eyes. God had looked favourably on her family. He had seen her. He had listened.

Moses went on.

'The Lord says we must give Zelo's daughters a grant of land along with their father's relatives. Assign them the property that would have been given to their father.'

One day a petition was presented by the daughters of Zelophehad—Mahlah, Noah, Hoglah, Milcah, and Tirzah. … These women stood before Moses, Eleazar the priest, the tribal leaders, and the entire community at the entrance of the Tabernacle. 'Our father died in the wilderness,' they said. … 'But he had no sons. Why should the name of our father disappear from his clan just because he had no sons?'…

So Moses brought their case before the Lord. And the Lord replied to Moses, 'The claim of the daughters of Zelophehad is legitimate. … Assign them the property that would have been given to their father.' (Numbers 27:1–7)

Collection

The bottles lined the wall, one shelf after another after another. Some bottles were only partly filled, and others were full right up to the brim. Some bottles were so large and so full that they almost touched the shelf above. He saw their height and he alone understood. He alone knew their weight.

They went on forever, so many bottles that it seemed they would never end.

But he held them all, regardless of their size. They were all accounted for. Collected by hand. They were all precious to him.

You keep track of all my sorrows. You have collected all my tears in your bottle. You have recorded each one in your book. (Psalm 56:8)

Alvan

It was earlier than usual for Alvan to be awake, but something had woken him. As a rooster, he was responsible for the protection of the flock. He jumped from his perch and landed with a flutter on the earth below. As far as he could tell, all was silent and calm, but why had he woken? He didn't know. He would take a walk and survey the area. If need be, he would sound the alarm.

Alvan didn't mind being woken early—he was a natural early riser, and the still of the morning was one of his favourite times. It prepared him for the chaos to come, once he had roused the rest of the brood.

There was a sound from among the flock. Alvan stood to attention, hoping he hadn't woken one of the chicks—waking one was as good as waking them all. No, it was one of the chickens. Alvan cocked his head to one side and watched to see who was waddling towards him. It was Ane. He liked Ane. She would come with him, and they would survey their surroundings for threats together. Alvan didn't have to tell Ane to stay quiet. She knew that it wasn't time for Alvan to wake the flock yet. It was too dark—much too early.

They waddled together around the edge of their field. All was calm and seemingly peaceful. Then Alvan spotted something above the treeline, a line of smoke trailing up into the sky. Ane and Alvan cocked their heads to one side as they watched the smoke. Smoke came from fire and fire usually came from humans, but what would humans be doing up so early? Alvan didn't know. He would take a look. Ane followed close behind him.

They scurried along the ground beneath the trees until they could hear the commotion up ahead. Alvan poked his head out from beneath a bush. Humans. He was right! He saw a group of them gathered around a fire. Some were seated while others stood. Ane poked her head out beside Alvan and they watched for a minute or so. The people held their hands before the fire to warm themselves as they spoke to each other.

This was unusual. The humans were meant to be sleeping, but today they were awake. It was too early, still much too dark, but perhaps he should sing his song anyway. Perhaps he should sound his alarm.

Alvan thought about it for a moment, then took a deep breath and crowed as loudly as he could, keeping his eyes on those gathered around the fire. As he drew his crow to a perfect finish, a young man swivelled on his heel and looked straight towards the trees where Alvan and Ane stood. He looked like he'd seen a ghost. Alvan wasn't used to the humans paying any attention to his song. Alvan looked from the man to Ane and back again. He cocked his head to one side and turned to head back to their field.

His work here was done.

But Jesus said, 'Peter, let me tell you something. Before the rooster crows tomorrow morning, you will deny three times that you even know me.' (Luke 22:34)

Meanwhile, as Simon Peter was standing by the fire warming himself, they asked him again, 'You're not one of his disciples, are you?'

He denied it, saying, 'No, I am not.'

But one of the household slaves of the high priest, a relative of the man whose ear Peter had cut off, asked, 'Didn't I see you out there in the olive grove with Jesus?' Again Peter denied it. And immediately a rooster crowed. (John 18:25–27)

Ozni

The tables were long and beautifully decorated. No expense had been spared, no detail forgotten. Ozni had never seen anything like it. The linen tablecloths were crisp and white, the flowers fresh, their scent heavenly. The candles down the centre of the table were all alight, and there was so much light.

Ozni wandered down alongside a table, resting her hands on the back of the chairs. They were wooden chairs, yet soft to her touch and inviting. She could smell food, something delicious. Her stomach rumbled. As she stopped and reached out to touch the rim of a crystal glass, she noticed a placard nestled into the greenery beside the cutlery. It had something printed on it and she squinted, leaning down to read it.

Ozni.

Breath caught in her throat when she realised it was her name. She whispered her name aloud. There was a place for her here. A place set for her.

In Jerusalem, the Lord of Heaven's Armies will spread a wonderful feast for all the people of the world.
It will be a delicious banquet with clear, well-aged wine and choice meat.
There he will remove the cloud of gloom, the shadow of death that hangs over the earth.

He will swallow up death forever! The Sovereign Lord will wipe away all tears. (Isaiah 25:6–8)

Noddy

Noddy was late. Of all mornings for Sela to have woken up ill, of course it had to be this morning. Sela looked dreadful and wasn't holding anything down, so Noddy had to bring their son along with him today. He huffed and puffed, dragging Pino along by the hand.

'Come on, boy,' Noddy said. 'We're already running late.' Noddy could see Pino was struggling to keep up—his little legs were moving as fast as they could go. Noddy sighed. It wasn't Pino's fault. Noddy felt bad and slowed down a little.

'Remember, we have an important meeting today. I don't want you getting in the way. You are to keep quiet, keep still, and behave.'

Pino nodded at his father. He was a good boy who knew his place, but Noddy couldn't have Pino mucking things up for them today. There was a plan in place. If all went well and Jesus performed the way they expected him to, then there would be hard evidence against him. It was all anybody in Noddy's circle talked about these days. Everybody was eager to see Jesus arrested.

Pino pulled his hand free from Noddy's and ran ahead. He'd obviously spotted something on the side of the road. He bent down and picked up a stick. That child! He was always collecting sticks. Pino turned back, grinning at Noddy as he held his stick up in the air to show him. Noddy was just about to tell him he couldn't bring it along, when Pino disappeared. He seemed to fall into thin air.

'Daaaad,' he called as he fell. Panicked, Noddy ran the small distance between them and saw Pino lying on his back at the bottom of a pit.

'Pino, are you ok?'

'I think so.' Pino whimpered and began to cry.

'Now, no time for that.' Noddy tried to keep the frustration out of his voice. They were already late, today of all days! 'Stand up and brush yourself off.'

Pino did as he was told, then reached up to grasp Noddy's outstretched hand. Noddy pulled him out of the pit and patted him on the shoulder. Pino's bottom lip quivered. Noddy needed Sela in situations like these. She always knew what to say to the child.

Noddy took hold of Pino's hand again and carried on. They were a little late arriving at Jerah's home, where the meal was being held, but it looked like everything was going to plan. Zebo—whom Noddy and his friends had hired—was in the dining room with Jesus.

Zebo's arms and legs were extremely swollen. No doubt Jesus would try to heal him. But then that's where it got tricky. It was illegal to work on the Sabbath—everyone knew that, though Jesus didn't seem to think the rules applied to him. So it would be interesting to see. Would he heal Zebo? Or would he obey the rules of the Sabbath and leave him be?

Pino sat in the corner of the room. Noddy would give him something to eat after everyone else had eaten. The boy had been quiet since his fall. His clothing was dirty, but Noddy was sure he was fine. Perhaps a little shocked. Noddy hoped Sela would be well enough to care for him on their return.

25

Jesus was talking to Zebo now, and Noddy tried to hear what it was they were saying. He raised his eyebrows at Jerah. This was it.

'Dad, I'm hungry.' Pino whispered in Noddy's ear.

'Ssshh!' Noddy wished Pino wasn't here. Jesus seemed to scan the dinner guests around the table, stopping when his eyes reached Jerah. Noddy held his breath.

'Is it permitted in the law to heal people on the Sabbath day, or not?' Jesus asked.

Noddy knew Jerah wouldn't answer. He knew because they were eager for Jesus to go ahead and heal Zebo. Besides, Jesus knew the law. He knew it wasn't permitted to work on the Sabbath, so why did he ask?

Pino still stood beside him. Noddy passed him a small slice of bread. 'Go back and sit in the corner,' he whispered.

Jerah gasped.

Had Noddy missed something? So much for Pino staying out of the way. Noddy stretched around the person beside him to see Zebo embracing Jesus, who laughed and patted his back. Zebo's arms and legs were restored to their regular size, the swelling completely gone. Jesus had done it.

Noddy and Jerah exchanged looks and Jerah shook his head. They had him now. There were many witnesses. Jesus had broken the law.

Jesus stood up from the table and led Zebo to the door. He seemed to be asking him to leave. When Jesus returned to the table, he looked at Noddy. Noddy wasn't sure why and busied himself filling up his plate. All the while, he could feel Jesus' eyes on him, so he put down his utensils and met Jesus' gaze. Jesus looked at him as though he could see more than Noddy wanted him to. Noddy squirmed in his seat.

'Which of you doesn't work on the Sabbath?' Jesus looked from Noddy to Jerah, then seemed to open his question to the room, but his eyes came back to Noddy's. Nobody answered him.

'If your son or your cow falls into a pit, don't you rush to get him out?' Jesus asked. This time he didn't take his eyes from Noddy. Noddy swallowed hard and felt the blood drain from his face. He felt a tugging on his arm.

'Dad, can I have another piece of bread?' Pino whispered.

One Sabbath day Jesus went to eat dinner in the home of a leader of the Pharisees, and the people were watching him closely. There was a man there whose arms and legs were swollen. Jesus asked the Pharisees and experts in religious law, 'Is it permitted in the law to heal people on the Sabbath day, or not?' When they refused to answer, Jesus touched the sick man and healed him and sent him away. Then he turned to them and said, 'Which of you doesn't work on the Sabbath? If your son or your cow falls into a pit, don't you rush to get him out?' (Luke 14:1–5)

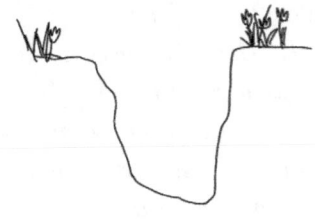

Ardo

Their time had come. Today was the day!

Ardo was just a stone who lived along the side of the road—they all were. But Ardo knew his place in creation, and he knew exactly what they were to do.

Ardo cleared his throat and waited until he had their full attention. All the stones looked to him. All eyes were on Ardo.

'Are you ready?' Ardo called out. 'Now remember—if they don't cry out, then it's up to us.' The stones were silent. They were always silent … that is, until today.

Ardo turned his attention back to the road. There were people everywhere, and God's son would arrive any minute.

'It's our time to shine,' Ardo whispered.

When they reached the place where the road started down the Mount of Olives, all of his followers began to shout and sing as they walked along, praising God for all the wonderful miracles they had seen.

'Blessings on the King who comes in the name of the Lord! Peace in heaven, and glory in highest heaven!'

But some of the Pharisees among the crowd said, 'Teacher, rebuke your followers for saying things like that!'

He replied, 'If they kept quiet, the stones along the road would burst into cheers!' (Luke 19:37–40)

Zarie

Zarie could tell her mother was scared. She was trying to pretend that she wasn't, but she was. Zarie watched her face through bleary eyes, eyes that were barely open. Her mother moved around the room, tight-lipped and fidgeting. She had dark circles under her eyes. Zarie wished she could jump up and wrap her arms around her mother and tell her she felt better now and they could go downstairs together, but instead Zarie shut her eyes.

Her head hurt. Everything hurt. The light made it hard to keep her eyes open. Zarie had never been sick like this before. She hoped she would be better soon. She wanted to ask where her father was, but she couldn't speak anymore. She hadn't spoken for a day or so now. Zarie wanted to cry, but she had grown so weak that only a single teardrop fell from the corner of her eye. Zarie was pleased her mother stood over by the window so she wouldn't see it.

Zarie's breathing was changing. She could feel the change but had no control over it. Her breaths came short and sharp and something shifted inside of her. She let out a small cry, then felt her mother's breath against her face and her mother's hand in hers. Tears dripped onto Zarie's face but, they were not her own.

'I love you, Zarie,' her mother whispered. She hadn't cried until now—at least, she hadn't cried in front of Zarie. 'My baby,' she whispered as she kissed Zarie's cheek and ran her hand over Zarie's forehead and down through her hair.

'Hold on, Zarie. Dad will be here soon.'

Zarie couldn't respond, although she wanted to—she wanted to tell her mother she was afraid, she needed her, she wanted to stay with her. But Zarie's eyes remained closed and her breathing became more shallow, until it stopped.

Zarie slowly floated up from the bed and found herself up high, looking down at her bed, at her body lying beneath the blankets, looking down at her mother hunched over her. Her mother was cradling Zarie's head and weeping into her hair.

Where was Zarie? Why could she see herself down there so clearly, and why did her mother wail so loudly?

Could she be dead?

Zarie was aware of a presence close beside her, just behind her, just to the left of her. Somebody was beside her, someone who knew her well. Zarie felt safe and known. She watched as events unfolded in her bedroom, down below.

Zarie's father came into the room and rushed to her mother's side. Zarie watched as he took her lifeless hand into his, holding it to his mouth as he wept. Another man followed her father into Zarie's bedroom, a stranger.

The stranger looked at Zarie's body lying on her bed, then looked up at Zarie. Could he see her, up there in the corner? He seemed to look right into her eyes. How surprising.

The stranger crossed the room to where Zarie's body lay and placed one hand on her. He took her hand in his, then looked up at where Zarie floated above them.

'My child, get up!' he said in a loud voice.

It was clear that whoever was beside Zarie was working with the stranger in her bedroom. Zarie felt as if she was slowly being taken back down to her bed and placed back inside her body. She opened her eyes. Her eyes no longer hurt and nor did her head. She sat straight up, and her parents jumped back. Zarie swung her legs off the bed and stood up for the first time in weeks. Her stomach grumbled as her parents embraced her.

'Give her something to eat,' the stranger said as he placed his hands on her parents' hunched shoulders. Zarie was alive.

Then Jesus took her by the hand and said in a loud voice, 'My child, get up!' and at that moment her life returned, and she immediately stood up! Then Jesus told them to give her something to eat. (Luke 8:54–5)

Lord,
let me
let you
love me.

Such love has no fear, because perfect love expels all fear.
If we are afraid, it is for fear of punishment, and this
shows that we have not fully experienced his perfect love.
(1 John 4:18)

Maly

Maly was the high priest's slave and he was cold tonight, but that didn't matter. He had an earache too. In fact, it had been sore all week, but that didn't matter either. He ran to keep up with his master, pulling his shirt tighter around his skinny frame.

They were headed to the olive grove, although Maly hadn't been informed of the evening's plan—why would he be? But he had picked up bits and pieces from conversations he overheard. From what he could gather, they were making an arrest.

Maly's sandals were growing too small and were rubbing against the side of his toe. He looked forward to lying down in his cot tonight to rest his aching ear and to take off his sandals. But he wasn't getting his hopes up that rest would come any time soon. By the looks of the size of their party of Roman soldiers and Pharisees, it was expected to be a difficult arrest.

Maly followed close behind his master, careful not to walk too fast in case he stepped on his master's sandal—Maly had suffered the consequences of that mistake before.

In one hand, he held his lantern high so the light helped brighten their path, and he held his shirt together with the other hand. A man Maly didn't know led the group. His name was Judas, and he looked like he knew exactly where he was going.

They crossed the Kidron Valley, then entered a grove of

olive trees. It seemed like a peaceful place—although the stomping feet of their party was in contrast to the setting. Maly stood on tiptoes to see over the soldiers' heads and could vaguely make out the shape of men up ahead among the trees. He hoped this would be quick. His earache was getting worse with the cold as the night became deeper.

'It's them. It's Jesus and his disciples,' Maly's master whispered.

Judas headed straight towards the group of men. Maly stood as tall as he could to see what would happen. The party came to a halt before Jesus and his disciples, but the high priest kept walking until he stood right beside Judas at the front of the group. Maly followed close behind, watching as Judas stepped forward and kissed Jesus on the cheek. How odd … perhaps this wasn't the man they were planning to arrest tonight after all. Maly looked from Jesus to Judas. There was silence.

'Judas, would you betray the Son of Man with a kiss?' Jesus asked, although his tone got Maly wondering if perhaps his question wasn't a question at all. Judas was stony-eyed and didn't flinch a muscle, though Maly sensed some discomfort.

Without warning, the men who were with Jesus—his disciples—drew their swords, the silver flashing against the dark night. Maly stepped behind his master, but his master yanked him back out to stand beside him. Maly would pay for that later.

'Lord, should we fight? We brought swords,' one of the disciples said.

No sooner had the words left his mouth than his sword was swinging through the air. It came crashing down beside Maly's head, cutting off his right ear. Maly fell to the ground, crying out in pain, and held his hand to his ear. His ear was gone, and blood covered his hand. His master called for the soldiers to release their weapons.

Somebody retrieved Maly's ear from the dirt and held it firmly against the side of his head. Maly grasped the man's hand and held it there. He felt sick to his stomach and thought he might pass out. There was blood everywhere. Would he bleed to death? What he would do to have his ear-ache back now!

Jesus crouched down beside Maly.

'No more of this.' His order seemed to be directed at his disciples. He placed a hand on Maly's shoulder, and Maly looked up into his face, afraid. What would Jesus do next?

Jesus held his other hand over Maly's and his dismembered ear. The world became quiet as Maly looked into Jesus' eyes. Maly sensed he should lower his hand, so he did, slowly pulling it away from his ear. Now only Jesus held his ear. A minute or so seemed to pass, as Jesus and Maly kneeled together, chaos around them. The space beneath Jesus' hand became very hot, as if it was on fire. Maly's eyes widened as the heat intensified then instantly cooled.

Jesus removed his hand and rose to his feet. Maly shot his hand up to his wound to find that there was no longer a wound. His ear was restored, completely—no pain, no cut, no blood whatsoever. Maly gasped, one hand over his restored ear. He lifted his head from the ground and watched Jesus as he stood between the soldiers and his disciples.

'Put away your sword,' Jesus told his disciples. 'Those who use the sword will die by the sword.' His disciples lowered their swords. 'Don't you realise that I could ask my Father for thousands of angels to protect us, and he would send them instantly? But if I did, how would the scriptures be fulfilled that describe what must happen now?'

But even as Jesus said this, a crowd approached, led by Judas, one of the twelve disciples. Judas walked over to Jesus to greet him with a kiss. But Jesus said, 'Judas, would you betray the Son of Man with a kiss?'

When the other disciples saw what was about to happen, they exclaimed, 'Lord, should we fight? We brought the swords!' And one of them struck at the high priest's slave, slashing off his right ear.

But Jesus said, 'No more of this.' And he touched the man's ear and healed him. (Luke 22:47–51)

Enough

He struggled to watch, and he said to the sun,
'That's enough now.'
And the sun replied,
'But it's too early.'
He shook his head, confirming his decision
'No. That's enough.'
So the sun disappeared.

At noon, darkness fell across the whole land until three o'clock. (Matthew 27:45)

Hattie

She'd done it! Hattie slumped into the chair beside her table and slowly exhaled. She was exhausted. The boys were hard work at the best of times, but when Zeru had to work late, they really pulled out all the stops for her. She'd got there in the end—now they were cleaned, fed, and in bed. Finally.

Hattie would get Zeru's dinner ready now. He would be tired after working such a long day. Her feet ached as she pulled herself up. She used her apron to wipe her brow and headed back into the kitchen. She prepared some bread and cheese and was just slicing the vegies when she heard Zeru at the front door. Hattie could tell he'd had a hard day as soon as she heard his work shoes hit the floor. He didn't call out to greet her as usual either. She braced herself.

'Hi, honey,' she called around the corner, trying to sound cheerful. 'How was your day?'

Zeru slumped into the same chair Hattie had just used, barely looking at her. 'I may not have a job anymore.'

Hattie could feel the blood drain from her face. She slowly crossed the room and took the seat beside him. She didn't speak, but waited for him to go on.

Zeru sighed, running his hands back over his forehead and through his hair. He looked her in the eyes. Finally.

'It was really bad, Hatt.'

She nodded, encouraging him on, and she reached out a hand to wrap around his.

'We disobeyed an order today.'

What? That could mean more than just losing his job. She tried not to cry.

'Why?' was all she could muster.

'That's the thing.' He shook his head and looked at the ground beneath his knees. 'I don't even know … I don't know what happened.' His words made no sense. But she didn't want to upset him further. She took a deep breath, trying to remain calm for the both of them.

'Start from the beginning,' she suggested. He nodded.

'They sent Tobi and I out to arrest a man today, a man named Jesus.' He dropped his head into his hands as he shook it and then sat back up. 'I can't figure out what happened. We found him quickly—he had a crowd of people gathered, listening to him—but that was the only easy part. The people were dead silent, as though mesmerised by his teachings, so we waited. Best to arrest him when he was finished, when there wasn't such a large audience to defend him.'

'Absolutely.' Hattie nodded. 'It wouldn't have been safe for you otherwise.' She wanted to hurry him along, to find out how the story ended. Had the crowd stood in their way and protected Jesus? Had he somehow slipped away and escaped them? She waited and listened.

Zeru looked into her eyes. Something had changed about him—his eyes were a million miles away.

'I couldn't do it,' he said simply. 'I have never heard anyone speak the way he spoke, and I just couldn't do it.' He'd been touched by the teacher's words? Hattie couldn't believe her ears.

'What did he say?' she asked.

Zeru didn't hesitate.

'He spoke about living water. I don't know what it is, but

he said that anyone who believed in him or anyone who was thirsty could go to him and drink.' Zeru was making no sense whatsoever.

'And?' Hattie asked.

'He said that the ancient scriptures spoke about him when it was written that rivers of living water would flow from his heart.'

Hattie wanted to yell at him. It sounded like he had risked his job, possibly even his life, because of something some man had said. What had happened to her husband? He sounded nothing like himself. She took a couple of deep breaths.

'I know it sounds crazy,' he said before she could speak. 'Like I say, I can't explain it.'

'What did you say to your superiors?' Hattie whispered. She braced herself for his reply.

'Well, we told them what I just told you—that we had never heard anyone speak like that.'

Hattie gulped over the lump that had formed in her throat.

On the last day, the climax of the festival, Jesus stood and shouted to the crowds, 'Anyone who is thirsty may come to me! Anyone who believes in me may come and drink! For the Scriptures declare, "Rivers of living water will flow from his heart."'

… When the Temple guards returned without having arrested Jesus, the leading priests and Pharisees demanded, 'Why didn't you bring him in?'

'We have never heard anyone speak like this!' the guards responded. (John 7: 37–38, 45–46)

Lilie

Lilie was a young wildflower who lived in a field of lilies. She was growing up beneath the sun, beside her mother. Lilie grew a little more every day. Some day she would stand as tall as her mother.

One morning, Lilie looked to her mother. 'Am I beautiful?' she asked. She had been wondering for many days.

'Oh yes. Didn't you know?' Her mother smiled down at Lilie, then stretched her face up towards the sun. 'God has dressed us beautifully, and he cares wonderfully for us.'

Lilie believed, and she followed her mother's lead, stretching her face as high as it would go towards the sun. She was beautiful.

'And why worry about your clothing? Look at the lilies of the field and how they grow. They don't work or make their clothing, yet Solomon in all his glory was not dressed as beautifully as they are. And if God cares so wonderfully for wildflowers that are here today and thrown into the fire tomorrow, he will certainly care for you. Why do you have so little faith?' (Matthew 6:28–30)

The Calling

The day had begun like any other. Simon and his brother Andrew were fishing on the Sea of Galilee as they always did. The sea was lapping at Simon's feet, and the sun shone down on top of his head. The wind rustled past his ears, and birds swooped down in hope of benefiting from their catch. Simon and Andrew didn't talk much today. Some days their work banter went on and on. Other days—like today—they were thoughtful, each man to himself.

Simon was tired. It had been building up inside of him for some time, and he knew he needed a rest. Fishing was his livelihood and he had always enjoyed it, but there had been a shift inside him recently. He sensed Andrew was feeling the same.

Simon rarely had time to stop and think. It wasn't until he was tucked up in bed that his mind was free to wander. Even then, Simon was exhausted from his work and was out like a light not long after his head hit the pillow.

There were questions that played in his mind each night. Was this all there was to life? Was fishing Simon's calling, his purpose? Given many months on repeat, what had begun as a small niggle, a quiet whisper, now felt more like a gaping hole and a raging question.

Simon wondered how he had felt such contentment in his life up until this point. More importantly, would he ever feel that contentment again?

He kept these thoughts to himself. He wasn't one to share, and he wasn't even sure what he would share if given the chance. But the restlessness was heavy today, so Simon stayed quiet.

Simon was pulled from his thoughts as Andrew threw the net towards him without warning. Simon caught it instinctively and laughed, while shaking his head.

'Nice try.'

Andrew shrugged. 'Somebody needed to wake you up.'

The brothers threw the net into the water. Simon straightened and pushed the hair back from his forehead when somebody walking along the shore caught his eye. It was the teacher, Jesus. He was a fascinating man.

Simon stopped and watched him. Andrew followed Simon's gaze. He grew quiet, standing and watching Jesus too. Simon's feet felt glued to the spot. It was rude to stare, but he couldn't have looked away even if he'd wanted to.

Jesus seemed to be walking straight towards them, his direction unfaltering. He stepped right up to where they fished. Simon's heart was beating harder than usual as he watched the teacher. Jesus stopped walking and looked into Simon's eyes. The breath caught in Simon's throat. What was going on here? Did the teacher have something to say?

Even as the questions formed in Simon's mind, a deep understanding, a belonging, welled up inside him, almost as though Simon had known Jesus would come. As though he'd been waiting for Jesus.

Jesus held his gaze for only a minute before he looked to Andrew. His eyes seemed to smile, and he looked back to Simon.

'Come, follow me, and I will show you how to fish for people,' Jesus said.

Fish for people? Simon's mind reeled. Come, follow him? What … right now? Just up and leave this very minute? And for what? To fish for people? That made no sense.

Simon was speechless. He looked from Jesus to Andrew, who hadn't taken his eyes from the teacher. Andrew dropped the net. Simon couldn't believe his eyes. He looked from Andrew's half of the net swaying in the water up into Jesus' eyes. Before he could grasp what was going on, his fingers loosened from the net and he dropped his half into the water too.

He had been called.

One day as Jesus was walking along the shore of the Sea of Galilee, he saw two brothers—Simon, also called Peter, and Andrew—throwing a net into the water, for they fished for a living. Jesus called out to them, 'Come, follow me, and I will show you how to fish for people!' And they left their nets at once and followed him. (Matthew 4:18–20)

The Linen Clothing

The linen clothing was taken off, hung in the sacred room and left alone. The door to the holy room closed. The linen clothing swayed just a little, back and forth, before finding its resting place. It hung still.

It was still, but it was not without life. Holiness remained within its fibres, deep into the night as it hung in the dark, sacred room.

The linen clothing had been worn in the presence of the living God. That type of thing was not to be taken lightly. It didn't wear off straight away. No, a residue of his presence remained. Because of this, the linen clothing could never be worn outside the doors, could never be witnessed by those beyond the sacred room. It wouldn't be safe.

When they enter the gateway to the inner courtyard, they must wear only linen clothing. They must wear no wool while on duty in the inner courtyard or in the Temple itself.

When they return to the outer courtyard where the people are, they must take off the clothes they wear while ministering to me. They must leave them in the sacred rooms and put on other clothes so they do not endanger anyone by transmitting holiness to them through this clothing. (Ezekiel 44:17, 19)

Hero

Hero loved to dance. She always had, ever since she was a child. She'd become obsessed with dancing after attending a wedding celebration where she had sat with her mother and father, watching the dancers perform. It was a special memory of a happy time before her parents had divorced. Hero had begun to dance then and had never stopped.

Hero had been preparing for months, and tonight was the night. Her stepfather, King Herod, was throwing a party for his high-ranking government officials, army officers, and the leading citizens of Galilee. It would be her largest performance yet, and the thought of those who would be present sent butterflies soaring through her stomach. Hero had never been so nervous in all her thirteen years. She could hardly eat. Now she stood in her room, knowing she was as ready as she would ever be, but she would practice again anyway. Hero put on her dancing shoes and pushed the furniture aside, performing her piece on the bedroom floor with her bed and dresser as her audience. Even she could tell it was a perfect performance.

She was ready.

The next few hours were full of makeup, hair braiding, and costumes. Hero's mother, the queen, had arranged for a brand new outfit for Hero to perform in. Hero looked at herself in the mirror, sure she had never looked so beautiful or so grown up. Her mother kissed her on the cheek before leaving the room.

'I'll see you out there, Hero. Good luck.' Her mother closed the door behind her. Hero took a couple of deep breaths, tightened her shoes, and with one last glance in the mirror, followed her mother out.

Hero cautiously entered the banquet hall. There were so many people gathered that Hero thought she might be sick. But she held her head up high, drawing strength from within. *You can do this.* She approached the head table and sat quietly beside her mother. Herod roared with laughter, and she could tell the wine was flowing. At least everyone would be in good spirits when her time came to perform.

Dinner was served, but Hero couldn't eat. She moved the food around her plate and sipped her mother's wine instead. The minutes crept by, until finally dessert was served and cleared. Then it was time for the entertainment to begin. Hero was relieved when they called her up first. She needed to get this done. Her pulse raced as she stepped onto the platform in front of King Herod and his friends. The audience quieted.

Hero could hardly breathe, but she stood in position, closed her eyes to centre herself, and began to move with the music. She was swept away as her love, her passion, for movement took over. When she opened her eyes, the crowd was still, completely silent, and all eyes were on Hero. Suddenly she remembered how much she loved this—how much she loved to be watched, to perform for an audience. She had forgotten.

Her piece drew to an end. With her final movement, the crowd erupted into applause. Herod roared above them all, and Hero couldn't contain her smile. She grinned from ear to ear, bowing her head to the left and to the right. Hero's mother was weeping, and it was clear everyone had enjoyed her performance. Her heart swelled with pride. She had done it.

Suddenly the crowd grew quiet again. King Herod had risen from his seat, holding his hands up and signalling for their silence. He looked straight at Hero, surprising her. What would he say? She held her breath. All eyes were on the king.

'Ask me for anything you like, and I will give it to you,' he said to Hero in front of the audience. Hero was stunned. What did he mean, anything? This was like something out of a dream. Anything that she would like?

'I will give you whatever you ask, up to half my kingdom!' He raised his hands higher. Tears sprung to Hero's eyes, and the crowd exploded into celebration.

'He is so generous,' someone called from the audience. Hero had never felt so treasured in all of her life. Her mind raced. What would she ask for? New dancing shoes, more costumes, perhaps even a dance studio, somewhere she could practice. Herod smiled at her.

'Go and discuss it with your mother, child. You don't need to decide this very minute.' Relief washed through her as she bowed her head and thanked him, then ran to her mother's side. Hero was surprised when her mother ushered her straight outside, exiting through a private side door, which the guards closed firmly behind them. Hero was on cloud nine as she turned to her mother, grinning from ear to ear.

'What should I ask for?' She was confused by the look on her mother's face, as though she were miles away. Her mother didn't smile at Hero, hug her, or congratulate her. The smile slowly faded from Hero's face.

'You must ask for the head of John the Baptist!' her mother replied.

For Herod had sent soldiers to arrest and imprison John as a favour to Herodias. She had been his brother Philip's wife, but Herod had married her. John had been telling Herod, 'It is against God's law for you to marry your brother's wife.' So Herodias bore a grudge against John and wanted to kill him. But without Herod's approval she was powerless.

Then his daughter, also named Herodias, came in and performed a dance that greatly pleased Herod and his guests. 'Ask me for anything you like,' the king said to the girl, 'and I will give it to you.'

She went out and asked her mother, 'What should I ask for?' Her mother told her, 'Ask for the head of John the Baptist!' (Mark 6:17–19, 22, 24)

Nova

Nova the star had been kept in the dark her entire life, and she never understood why. Those around her twinkled and shone almost as bright as the sun while Nova sat in the background, watching them. She was unseen and unnoticed, but he whispered to her.

Your time will come.

He had created Nova, so she believed him, and she waited. But time passed slowly. Night after night and year after year, Nova watched them shine, and night after night and year after year, she was reminded of the darkness that surrounded her.

Then one night, he called to her. Nova could hardly believe what she heard.

Come.

It was a simple command, and she followed the sound of his voice. Nova was placed in the night sky where she shone for the first time in her life. Nova shone brighter than all the other stars around her. She followed his whispers, concentrating on the sound of his voice. She made her way across the sky until she rested above Bethlehem, above a stable.

... About that time some wise men from eastern lands arrived in Jerusalem, asking, 'Where is the newborn king of the Jews? We saw his star as it rose, and we have come to worship him.'

... And the star they had seen in the east guided them to Bethlehem. It went ahead of them and stopped over the place where the child was. When they saw the star, they were filled with joy! (Matthew 2:1–2, 9–10)

Kiah

Kiah had never been so sick in his entire life. He felt pain everywhere. It even hurt to breathe. He lay in his bed, watching the prophet's face. Kiah knew Isaiah the prophet could hear from the living God, and wondered if Isaiah might have come to visit for another reason besides his gift of water and flowers. Perhaps Isaiah had a message for him from God. Maybe Isaiah was here to tell Kiah that he would recover soon, and all would be well.

It hurt to keep his eyes open. Kiah blinked a couple of times and focused on Isaiah, waiting.

'I have a message for you from the Lord, Kiah,' Isaiah said.

Kiah had been right! What would the message be? Kiah's palms grew clammy and he gripped the blanket beside him.

'This is what the Lord says: set your affairs in order, for you are going to die. You will not recover from this illness.'

Kiah felt like the breath had been knocked from his lungs. He gasped and closed his eyes, and the room seemed to spin. Kiah was taken back to a memory from his childhood, to the time when he had first encountered the Spirit of God. Kiah remembered the feeling as though it had been yesterday. He had experienced the God of Israel and had discovered the Lord was kind, so very kind. Kiah had served God his entire life, with all of his heart and all of his strength.

Isaiah touched Kiah's arm, and the prophet left the room. Kiah rolled over in his bed, facing the wall beside his head and opened his eyes. He held his face close to the wall, and tears streamed down his cheeks. His mind reeled. Could it really be true? But he knew the answer. He knew Isaiah heard directly from God.

'Remember, O my Lord, how I have always been faithful to you,' he whispered to the wall. 'Remember how I have served you single-mindedly, always doing what pleases you.' Kiah had more to say, but his words were washed away as he wept bitter, gut-wrenching sobs that came from his very core. Kiah felt like his heart might break. He was not ready to die.

Minutes passed and Kiah heard somebody enter the room. He remained still and facing the wall, hoping whoever it was would just go away. His head hurt terribly, and now he knew he would never recover, he would never be well again. He lay still, as tears fell silently onto his pillow.

But whoever it was didn't leave. Instead, the person stood silently, waiting for Kiah. Kiah finally turned in his bed and was shocked to see Isaiah was back.

'What is it?' Surely there wasn't more? It couldn't get any worse than it already was. Isaiah stepped further into the room and closer to Kiah's bed.

'The Lord has sent me back.'

Kiah's mind reeled. Why would God send Isaiah back?

'His message is this,' Isaiah said. 'I have heard your prayer and seen your tears. I will heal you, and three days from now you will get out of bed and go to the temple of the Lord. I will add fifteen years to your life.'

Kiah couldn't breathe. God had listened to him? God had heard his whispers to the wall? Kiah's prayer had changed the mind of the living God? Kiah wanted to jump up and wrap his arms around Isaiah. Instead, he closed his aching eyes and a steady flow of tears streamed down his face.

Kiah would live. God heard him. Kiah's prayers mattered to God.

But before Isaiah had left the middle courtyard, this message came to him from the Lord: 'Go back to Hezekiah, the leader of my people. Tell him, "This is what the Lord, the God of your ancestor David, says: I have heard your prayer and seen your tears. I will heal you, and three days from now you will get out of bed and go to the Temple of the Lord. I will add fifteen years to your life."' (2 Kings 20:4–6)

Cold

It was cold that night. Were you cold?

Did you notice the temperature? Did you shiver? Did your skin prickle? Or was the fear so heavy, the pain so sharp, that all instincts were lost?

Did your feet ache on the ground as you stood there, early that morning? Were they chilled to the bone, or did they throb from the heat of your wounds?

So very alone, Lord, with no one who cared for your well-being, no one who cared for your body, for your comfort.

Were you cold, Lord?

Because it was cold, the household servants and the guards had made a charcoal fire. They stood around it, warming themselves, and Peter stood with them, warming himself. (John 18:18)

Bea

They were going to kill her baby. Bea held him tight and ran from her house. Her feet were bare. No time to put on sandals.

They were close, in her neighbour's home. She could hear their screams. Blood-curdling screams, of a mother whose child has been ripped from her arms.

Bea's son was three months old, and she had managed to keep him hidden until now. She was unable to let him go without a fight, her love for him too fierce.

Bea had prepared for this moment as best she could. She had a plan. A plan that would break her heart, but it was all she had—her only hope, and his only chance of survival. Her project had taken her many weeks—a basket made of papyrus reeds, and waterproofed with tar and pitch.

The basket was where she'd left it, hidden between the reeds on the bank of the Nile River. She was relieved to see it.

She lifted it from its hiding place.

He squirmed, moving his head against her chest and she felt sick. Would she be able to do this? How would she ever actually let him go?

Her eyes filled with tears, and she sat down on the bank beside the river. She unwrapped him from his hiding place and held her face close to his. She kissed his forehead and inhaled deeply of his skin as her tears fell.

'Protect him, God. Go before him. Lead him to safety. Rescue him from the hands of Pharaoh. I give him to you.

I place him in your care. God, let my baby live.' The words came out in sobs as Bea wrapped him snuggly in his blanket.

She didn't let herself think of the depths of the river or the terrors that could be found there. Instead she repeated her prayer, over and over.

She kissed his eyelids one last time, thankful that he slept, yet aware that she may never again see the colour of his eyes or the way they looked into hers. She placed him tenderly into the basket and closed the lid.

Footsteps sounded behind Bea. She jumped to her feet. She had to let him go now, before they arrived and stopped her. She placed the basket between the reeds, setting it afloat on the river.

'Mama,' Shilo called. Bea let out a breath of relief. It was her daughter. Shilo must have followed her. Bea dropped to her knees, welcoming Shilo into her arms. Shilo was safe. There was no threat to her life, because she was a girl.

'Where is he?' Shilo whispered against her mother's neck. Bea held her finger to her lips and pulled back the reeds beside them. The basket had drifted almost out of reach. No! She wanted to keep him close, wanted to reach out and pull him back while she still could. But there was no other way. This was the plan, and she must let him go.

Shilo cried as they watched the basket toss to and fro with the river. 'Won't he be hungry? Won't he be scared?' Shilo buried her face into Bea's chest, sobbing. 'I love him.'

Bea held her tears. She had to.

'We have to trust God, Shilo,' she whispered as she held Shilo close. Bea's words were as much for herself as they were for her daughter. 'God has a plan for his life.'

'I love you, my baby,' Shilo whispered out over the river to her brother.

Then Pharaoh gave this order to all his people: 'Throw every newborn Hebrew boy into the Nile River. But you may let the girls live.'

About this time, a man and woman from the tribe of Levi got married. The woman became pregnant and gave birth to a son. She saw that he was a special baby and kept him hidden for three months. But when she could no longer hide him, she got a basket made of papyrus reeds and waterproofed it with tar and pitch. She put the baby in the basket and laid it among the reeds along the bank of the Nile River. The baby's sister then stood at a distance, watching to see what would happen to him. (Exodus 1:22 & 2:1–4)

The Great Escape

It had been a wild day and the sea was restless. The weather seemed unable to decide which way it would go, so the sea, in turn, was unsettled. It tossed this way and that, forming large waves that crashed into one another and sent mist flying into the sky.

There was a sound. Someone was approaching.

The earth vibrated with the sound of many feet hitting the soil, and the sea paused and watched. Who could it be at this time of the morning? Who approached the sea's great shoreline and where did they plan to go?

It was a great sea of people, hundreds of thousands of people, all following their leader, all walking towards the sea. The sea froze and stood to attention.

'It is the people of the Lord. Quickly, move. Get out of their way,' the sea called. 'They belong to him, let them past.'

When the Israelites escaped from Egypt—when the family of Jacob left that foreign land—The Red Sea saw them coming and hurried out of their way! (Psalm 114:1, 3)

Let seeking your face be more important to me than
the upkeep of mine.

*Don't store up treasures here on earth, where moths eat
them and rust destroys them, and where thieves break in
and steal. Store your treasures in heaven, where moths
and rust cannot destroy, and thieves do not break in and
steal. Wherever your treasure is, there the desires of your
heart will also be.* (Matthew 6:19–21)

Sunny

Sunny had passed from life into death, that much he knew for sure. Nothing was as it had been. Sunny was moving, but wasn't aware how and didn't know where to.

There was a temple up ahead of him, very large and very grand. It glistened in the sunlight, although there was no sun above him as far as Sunny could tell. Perhaps the light came from somewhere else. A large wall surrounded the temple area, and Sunny felt drawn towards it. He would go inside. He would enter through the wall. He would go to the temple. Sunny stood before the wall admiring its magnificence and wondering at its size. Words washed over him.

'Ten and a half feet high and ten and a half feet thick'.

And then he knew.

Sunny arrived at the gateway beyond the wall. He floated up the steps, past the guard alcoves built into the gateway passage, past the gateway's inner threshold. The entry room was just up ahead … but how did he know that?

Windows lined the walls and there were palm tree decorations on the columns. Sunny silently observed the temple details, taking them all in, piece by piece, detail by precious detail. With each new detail, words washed over him. They were measurements.

'Ten and a half feet thick, ten and a half feet high. Ten and a half feet front to back. Ten and a half feet square. A distance between of eight and three-quarter feet.' The measurements kept coming, on and on.

Sunny didn't understand why the measurements were important, or why he needed to know them. But what he did know, what he was sure of, was that he would find out.

In a vision from God he took me to the land of Israel and set me down on a very high mountain. From there I could see toward the south what appeared to be a city. As he brought me nearer, I saw a man whose face shone like bronze standing beside a gateway entrance. He was holding in his hand a linen measuring cord and a measuring rod.

I could see a wall completely surrounding the Temple area. The man took a measuring rod that was 10 ½ feet long and measured the wall, and the wall was 10 ½ feet thick and 10 ½ feet high. (Ezekiel 40:2–3, 5)

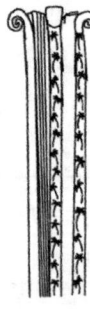

Seen

You see me.
What I do and where I go matter to you.
I am not just one in a crowd.

> *O Lord, you have examined my heart*
> *and know everything about me.*
> *You know when I sit down or stand up.*
> *You know my thoughts even when I'm far away.*
> (Psalm 139:1–2)

Lizy

Lizy sat on the couch with her legs folded beneath her, her swelling belly resting on her thighs. She took a deep breath before sipping her hot drink. She was tired, tired but full of joy. Some days, Lizy was still in shock at the way her life had changed. By her calculations, she was now six months pregnant. That in itself was a miracle! Lizy was well past the age of childbearing, and had never fallen pregnant like her sisters.

But now, here she was, pregnant. It was like something out of a dream. Lizy ran her free hand over her abdomen. She loved him already. It was extraordinary. She had always wondered what it would be like, to hold another within her body. Now that she knew, her eyes filled with tears, as they so often did these days.

'Thank you,' she whispered. It was all she could do some days; all she could say. Her whispered word hung in the air. She felt so close to God, almost as if she would be able to hear him if she were just quiet enough. Lizy smiled to herself and took another sip from her cup. Lizy's husband would be home soon, and she needed to finish preparing dinner. A couple more minutes and she would get up.

Footsteps approached the front door. Perhaps he was home early. Lizy placed her cup down on the table and prepared to rise when the door burst open.

Mary! Lizy's cousin. What was she doing here?

Lizy's baby shook inside her abdomen, an unexpected,

violent movement, as though he had somersaulted clear over. Lizy held both hands over her belly in shock and cried out as fear and wonder fell over her. She stood from the couch and looked up from her stomach into Mary's eyes. Mary's face was alight as though filled with excitement, and joy radiated from her eyes.

Lizy felt the words bubbling up within her involuntarily before she had a chance to think about their meaning.

'God has blessed you above all women, and your child is blessed.'

Mary's eyes filled with tears and she held her hands over her abdomen. Could it be true? Was Mary also expecting a child?

'Why am I so honoured, that the mother of my Lord should visit me?' The words were new to Lizy, as though they were not her own, as though they were given to her. She felt him near, closer than her breath.

Lizy paused, trying to get a hold of what was going on, looking from Mary's belly and then down to her own.

'Mary …' Lizy said. 'When I heard your greeting, the baby in my womb jumped for joy.'

At the sound of Mary's greeting, Elizabeth's child leaped within her, and Elizabeth was filled with the Holy Spirit.

Elizabeth gave a glad cry and exclaimed to Mary, 'God has blessed you above all women, and your child is blessed. Why am I so honored, that the mother of my Lord should visit me? When I heard your greeting, the baby in my womb jumped for joy. You are blessed because you believed that the Lord would do what he said.' (Luke 1:41–45)

65

Freedom

The sky was full of clouds. There were large clouds and small clouds. Dense clouds and thin clouds. Some were heavy and others light, some were dark and others white.

The artist took his hand and swept the sky. In one swift movement, the clouds were gone and the sky was clear.

I, the Lord, made you, and I will not forget you.
I have swept away your sins like a cloud.
I have scattered your offenses like the morning mist.
Oh, return to me, for I have paid the price to set you free.
(Isaiah 44:21–22)

The Catch-Up

Moses and Elijah had been sent from heaven to meet with Jesus. It was almost time for it to happen—the end of Jesus' life on earth—and there were things to discuss. They met him on a mountain.

Jesus had brought along some friends. They were asleep, which was a good thing, considering the circumstances. Moses watched Jesus closely as Elijah spoke. Jesus seemed calm. They all knew of the days he had ahead—they would be big days, they would be hard days. Moses didn't envy him. He admired Jesus greatly, but didn't envy him. If anybody could endure what lay ahead though, it was Jesus. He was his Father's son and was so much like his Father that Moses recognised him in Jesus' words each time he spoke. Their likeness was quite extraordinary.

Moses listened intently to the discussion going back and forth between Jesus and Elijah. He added a thing or two but mostly observed. Moses wasn't a big talker. He heard a shuffle behind him and realised that Jesus' friends had woken. They would be overwhelmed.

Elijah nodded at Moses. It was time for them to leave. Moses reached out a hand and held Jesus firmly by the shoulder and looked into his eyes, a look that spoke the many words he could not, a look that said, 'I stand with you.'

Elijah and Moses turned to leave.

'Master,' one of Jesus' friends blurted out. All three men turned to face him. 'It's wonderful for us to be here!'

It was clear the young man was in shock.

'Let us make three shelters as memorials—one for you, one for Moses, and one for Elijah,' the friend said.

In an instant, God covered Moses, Elijah, and Jesus with a thick cloud, so they were no longer visible to the young men.

'This is my Son, my chosen one. Listen to him,' God said from the cloud.

Moses and Elijah smiled at Jesus and departed.

Jesus now stood alone on the mountain with his friends. He knelt beside them, reassuring them.

'I don't know what I was thinking, blurting that out.' Peter shook his head, embarrassed. Jesus laughed and pulled him to his feet.

Peter blurted out, 'Lord, it's wonderful for us to be here! If you want, I'll make three shelters as memorials—one for you, one for Moses, and one for Elijah.'

He said this because he didn't really know what else to say, for they were all terrified. (Matthew 17:4, Mark 9:6)

Junia

Neko had asked for some bread. He was hungry after spending his morning running around with the other children in the neighbourhood. Junia went into the kitchen to prepare him a snack. He wanted bread, did he? Well, Junia would show him what she thought about that.

She fetched a small plate from below her bench, then stepped outside into the sunshine where she followed the path down to the roadside. She knelt, observing the stones until she found the perfect one. It was actually shaped a bit like a small slice of bread. That was fitting!

Junia picked it up and walked back inside, turning the stone over in the palm of her hand until she was back in the kitchen. She placed the stone on Neko's plate and found him sitting at the dining room table. He was obviously famished, but waiting patiently. He was a good boy.

'Thank you, Mama,' he said excitedly as she entered the room. Junia patted his head and placed the plate before him.

Junia watched his face as confusion settled in. He looked from the stone up into her eyes. She didn't say a word.

'It's a stone, Mama,' he finally said.

'Yes.' Junia nodded. 'It's a stone. Now eat it.' She said as she left the room.

You parents—if your children ask for a loaf of bread, do

you give them a stone instead? Or if they ask for a fish, do you give them a snake? Of course not! So if you sinful people know how to give good gifts to your children, how much more will your heavenly Father give good gifts to those who ask him. (Matthew 7:9–11)

David

David's heart beat heavily against his chest. He couldn't believe what Nathan had told him. Just the day before, David's thoughts had been consumed with building the Lord a new home, of replacing his tent with a palace. But this morning Nathan had brought David a message from the Lord, a message that had blown David's mind.

David would not be the one to build God a home, but God would build David a home. God would build David a lasting dynasty. The promises Nathan revealed that the Lord had spoken over David were unbelievable. David hurried down to the Lord's tent. He needed to speak with him.

He stopped just outside the entrance and took a deep breath before pulling back the cover. He stepped silently inside and crossed the floor. David sat down before the Lord, crossed his legs and held his head in his hands. He looked down to the floor through his fingers; there was dust and dirt beneath his legs. He sniffed loudly and lifted his head. He could hardly swallow over the lump that had formed in his throat. He didn't understand why.

Why did he, of all people, deserve this? What had he ever done to deserve such goodness, such divine privilege? He couldn't comprehend it. The promises were too much, they were overwhelming. He dropped his head back down into his hands and could barely make out the dirt beneath his folded legs now. Tears fell from his face, hitting the ground around his sandals.

'Lord.' His voice shook. 'Who am I and what is my family that you have brought me this far?' He shook his head in utter disbelief and pushed the hair back from his face. He boldly looked up. Nathan's words played over in David's mind.

'*I took you from tending sheep in the pasture and selected you to be the leader of my people, Israel. Now I will make your name as famous as anyone who has ever lived on earth.*'

'And now, Sovereign Lord, in addition to everything else, you speak of giving your servant a lasting dynasty!' He shook his head, speechless. 'You speak as though I were someone very great O Lord God, do you deal with everyone in this way?'

His question hung in the air. David rocked back and forth, pulling his legs up and holding them close to his body. What had he done to deserve this? How could he ever thank God? What could he ever say that would be enough?

Minutes passed, and the silence surrounded him.

'What more can I say to you?' David finally whispered. 'You know what your servant is really like.' Tears welled again. David was so far from perfect, so very far from holiness. And yet God had chosen him. Somehow God had loved him enough to choose him.

David sat back and crossed his legs once more before him. He cleared his throat, trying to regain composure. 'How great you are, O Sovereign Lord! There is no one like you, there is no one like you.' He shook his head. He meant every word.

Then King David went in and sat before the Lord and prayed,

'Who am I, O Sovereign Lord, and what is my family, that you have brought me this far? And now, Sovereign Lord, in addition to everything else, you speak of giving your servant a lasting dynasty! Do you deal with everyone this way, O Sovereign Lord?

'What more can I say to you? You know what your servant is really like, Sovereign Lord.' (2 Samuel 7:18–20)

Our Place

There's a secret place where I meet with you.
I can't see it with my physical eyes.
But one day you'll show it to me.
I'll know when I see it—
It was the place where we met together.
I'll recognise it as the place where you whispered to me.
The place where you revealed truths. About myself.
About you.
The place where you prepared me to fight against his lies.
The place where we were just 'us'.
Away from the crowds, away from the world.
Although I couldn't see it, it was the realest place of all.

*Then Jesus said, 'Come to me, all of you who are weary
and carry heavy burdens, and I will give you rest. Take my
yoke upon you. Let me teach you, because I am humble
and gentle at heart, and you will find rest for your souls.
For my yoke is easy to bear, and the burden I give you is
light.'* (Matthew 11:28–30)

Zabel

Zabel was beautiful and she knew it. As a child, she hadn't understood why people stared or why she drew so much attention. But she had learned, and with age, Zabel had become even more beautiful. She had grown into her larger-than-life features. Her beauty became both her greatest asset and her greatest curse.

When Zabel turned thirteen and was of age, many men had wanted to marry her. Jehd was wealthy and had paid Zabel's mother a considerable amount for her hand. Zabel's mother, a prostitute, had been unable to decline. As a child, Zabel had seen many men come into her home, then leave as fast as they'd arrived. Her mother's profession had taught her much about men.

Zabel was not ready for marriage and had found it difficult to adjust to her new life as Jehd's wife. At fourteen, she was approached by Jehd's Uncle Ty. Ty told her of her beauty, that he had never met anyone like her. Perhaps she had craved Ty's attention after having no father of her own. Perhaps Ty should have known better, being thirty years her senior, but Zabel had not. So she'd left Jehd and married Ty. At the time, Zabel was sure it was the right decision. It didn't take long for her to learn of Ty's other mistresses. It seemed Zabel wasn't the only one Ty found irresistible.

Zabel had met Timmy in the marketplace around that time. He'd been buying vegetables and had stopped in his tracks with his mouth hanging open, staring at Zabel. This in itself wasn't uncommon, but there was something about his eyes. She had felt drawn to them. Perhaps it was just the fact that they looked at her—Ty's eyes had wandered months before. Timmy had a mischievous smile and before Zabel knew it, he had swept her off her feet.

After leaving Ty and marrying Timmy, Zabel had been happy for many months. Timmy loved her—she was sure of that. But their love seemed to fizzle out almost as fast as it began. Zabel found herself responding to the attention of other males in town.

It wasn't long before she'd been approached by Odie at Mount Gerazim and had felt a connection. Odie had confessed his feelings for Zabel and she'd known he was married. But she had also known—more than most—that marriage wasn't final. And who was she to judge whether Odie had truly loved his wife? At least, that was how she justified it. Odie asked her to marry him and Zabel had been powerless to refuse. Love had taken over.

Zabel's marriage with Odie was the longest of her marriages. She had been sure that their marriage would last. But then there was Ziel. Ziel was Odie's best friend. Ziel kissed Zabel one evening when dark fell and she realised, quite instantly, that Ziel was the missing part of her heart.

They hadn't married yet, but Zabel was sure when they did, that things would go well for them.

The women in town didn't like Zabel. They crossed to the other side of the road when she walked past and would steer their husbands clear of her. Zabel could see what they thought of her. A part of her understood. A part of her ached to be included. But as long as she had Ziel, he was all that she needed now.

Zabel pretended it didn't bother her, that she didn't notice the way she was never invited when the women gathered together. Zabel was not welcome.

For this reason, Zabel would wait until the other women had collected their water from the well before leaving to collect her own. The women walked together in the morning, chatting and laughing as they went. Zabel waited until the middle of the day, when she was sure she would be alone.

Today was hot. Zabel would need to rest at the well. But when she arrived, there was already a man resting at the well, a Jew. Zabel was taken by surprise. Instead of joining him, she got busy drawing her water. She didn't look at the stranger. Better to mind her own business and leave as quickly as she could.

As Zabel filled her containers, she could feel the stranger's eyes on her. The attention made Zabel uncomfortable, mainly because she wasn't prepared for it. She was well-used to men admiring her rare beauty—but not here, at the well. This was the women's place. Zabel worked as fast as she could, then turned to leave.

'Please give me a drink,' the stranger asked.

Zabel swivelled on her heel to face the stranger and looked into his face for the first time. He was clearly a Jew, so why was he speaking to her? Was water all he was after? Jews refused to speak to Samaritans. Had Zabel's beauty crossed the barrier between their differences? Zabel had been approached by many men but never by a Jew.

'You are a Jew.' Zabel finally found her voice. 'I am a Samaritan woman. Why are you asking me for a drink?'

That should shut him down. Bring the stranger to his senses. He shouldn't be speaking to her.

The stranger didn't respond. Instead, he looked at Zabel

and his silence was unnerving. Who was this man? And why did Zabel feel an odd familiarity when she looked in his eyes?

'If you only knew the gift God has for you, and who you are speaking to, you would ask me, and I would give you living water.'

Living water? What was that? He was obviously out of his mind.

'But, sir, you don't have a rope or a bucket.' Zabel tried to speak politely, aware they were alone. If he was crazy, Zabel would need to make a run for it. 'The well is very deep. Where would you get this living water? Besides, do you think you're greater than our ancestor Jacob, who gave us this well? How can you offer better water than he and his sons and his animals enjoyed?' Her words sounded harsher than she had intended, but they were out now.

The stranger smiled at Zabel.

'Anyone who drinks this water will soon become thirsty again. But those who drink the water I give will never be thirsty again. It becomes a fresh, bubbling spring within them, giving them eternal life.'

Something stirred deep inside of Zabel as she listened. Odd. Could there ever be a water like the one he described? Surely not. But if there was, she wanted it.

'Please, sir, give me this water. Then I'll never be thirsty again, and I won't have to come here to get water.'

The stranger was silent again, looking deep into Zabel's eyes.

'Go and get your husband,' he finally said.

'I don't have a husband,' Zabel replied. It was the truth, at least for now.

'You're right.' Jesus nodded. Zabel raised her eyebrows, surprised. 'You don't have a husband—for you have had five husbands, and you aren't even married to the man you're living with now.' He spoke gently this time, his words touching Zabel, hitting a spot deep inside her. She looked up at the stranger, tears forming in her eyes, her vision blurred.

'You certainly spoke the truth,' he said.

Zabel couldn't breathe. How did he know these things about her? Who was this man?

Zabel learned his name—Jesus. She spoke to Jesus a while longer, then ran as fast as she could back into town, where she told her story to anybody who would listen.

'His name is Jesus and he told me everything I ever did.'

Jacob's well was there; and Jesus, tired from the long walk, sat wearily beside the well about noontime. Soon a Samaritan woman came to draw water, and Jesus said to her, 'Please give me a drink.' He was alone at the time because his disciples had gone into the village to buy some food.

The woman was surprised, for Jews refuse to have anything to do with Samaritans. She said to Jesus, 'You are a Jew, and I am a Samaritan woman. Why are you asking me for a drink?'

Many Samaritans from the village believed in Jesus because the woman had said, 'He told me everything I ever did!' (John 4:6–9, 39)

Enemy

He feeds me lies and I believe them.

But you tilt my chin towards you, and the world becomes quiet. You tell me:

'You are mine. Just look at me. Don't look to the left or to the right. Accept my fresh mercy each morning. Because he's a liar, and he has no power over you.'

When he lies, it is consistent with his character; for he is a liar and the father of lies. (John 8:44)

'For I know the plans I have for you,' says the Lord. 'They are plans for good and not for disaster, to give you a future and a hope.' (Jeremiah 29:11)

Obi

Obi had witnessed crucifixions before, but none like this. He'd arrived late, because he'd been helping his sister move furniture.

Obi was curious and didn't want to miss this crucifixion. He ran up the hill and pushed through the crowd, making his way to the front. He was just in time to see the Roman soldiers lift the crosses from the ground. The soldiers guarded the base and he could go no further.

There were three men being crucified today. Obi had heard rumours about Jesus, the one nailed to the middle cross.

Obi was dubious about whether to believe the things he'd heard. He hadn't seen Jesus perform a miracle and he was far from gullible. But at the same time, he couldn't imagine why so many people would lie about the things they claimed they'd seen. The people around Obi were loud, hollering and mocking the condemned men.

'If you are the king of the Jews, save yourself now. Then we'll believe in you,' one man yelled from the crowd. Others laughed in agreement.

Jesus was covered in dried blood from head to toe, and a sign hung above his head, saying 'King of the Jews'.

'So you're the Messiah, are you?' the criminal who hung on the cross beside Jesus called out. 'Prove it by saving yourself—and us too, while you're at it!' Jesus stood up on the nails through his ankles, lifting himself to breathe, then dropped down again. It looked excruciating, and Obi found it hard to watch.

The sun beat down on the crowd, and Obi grew hot and restless. He held up his hands to shade his face, keeping his eyes on Jesus.

At noon, the sun disappeared. It had been a clear day, and it turned to darkness within a matter of minutes. It was eerily dark, as though night were approaching too soon.

Obi was sure that much time hadn't passed. His stomach grumbled. He hadn't even had lunch, and it was still many hours from nightfall.

'Why is it so dark?' Obi overheard a woman ask. The people were whispering around him, and he sensed a deep fear settle over the crowd. Something unusual was happening. Surely the darkness couldn't have anything to do with Jesus. Obi shuddered at the thought.

Hours passed, and the sun didn't return. If anything, it became darker. Now Obi could only make out the shadow of the three crosses before him. He watched as Jesus heaved himself up for air again, then fell back down. He seemed to be growing tired. Something was changing.

'My God,' Jesus called out. 'My God, why have you abandoned me?' Obi jumped back, knocking the person who stood behind him.

'Excuse me.' He turned back to face Jesus.

Obi spotted a jar of wine and a sponge beside the soldier at the base of the cross. Jesus must be thirsty, and he wanted to help. His heart raced as he crouched down to the ground in search of a stick. The darkness made it hard to see, but Obi spotted a reed stick between the legs of a bystander. He pulled it through the dust towards him. Obi stood up. Holding the stick, he approached the stern-faced soldier.

'Can I offer him some wine?' Obi pointed to the jar. The soldier stared at Obi, his face as unresponsive as stone. A strong sense of purpose came over Obi, prompting his spirit. He needed to offer Jesus the wine, regardless of the soldier's response. Obi was there for a reason.

He slowly stepped forward, not breaking eye contact with the soldier. Step by step, he made his way to the wine jar. It was the bravest thing he had ever done.

Obi attached the sponge to the end of his stick and then dipped it into the wine, careful not to make any sudden movements. He was surprised the soldier did nothing to stop him. Perhaps the soldier was afraid himself? After all, it was too dark for this time of the day.

Obi waited until the sponge was soaked through, then stood directly under the feet of Jesus. The soldier rushed to his side, as though waking from a trance. He would make sure Obi didn't try to rescue Jesus from his cross.

Obi lifted the stick up high and directed it to Jesus' lips, trying to be gentle. When it touched his lips, Jesus lifted his head, opened his eyes, and looked up to the heavens.

'It is finished!' he called out. Obi jumped back, taking the stick with him. He kept his eyes on Jesus. As he watched Jesus' face, Obi could see Jesus had gone. His spirit had left his body.

At noon, darkness fell across the whole land until three o'clock. At about three o'clock, Jesus called out with a loud voice, 'My God, my God, why have you abandoned me?' Some of the bystanders misunderstood and thought he was calling for the prophet Elijah. One of them ran and filled a sponge with sour wine, holding it up to him on a reed stick so he could drink. But the rest said, 'Wait! Let's see whether Elijah comes to save him.'

Then Jesus shouted out again, and he released his spirit. (Matthew 27:45–50)

Substance: our prayers are incense in golden bowls.

And when he took the scroll, the four living beings and
the twenty-four elders fell down before the Lamb. Each
one had a harp, and they held gold bowls filled with
incense, which are the prayers of God's people.
(Revelation 5:8)

A Mother's Treasure

29 March. It's late, and we've just arrived home. I should head to bed, but I need to get this out of my head and onto paper.

It feels like my spirit is bubbling inside me, as though it might burst. What does this all mean? Who is my baby boy? And what will become of him?

Most days he is just my boy, and I know everything about him, like the back of my hand. Most of the time I can guess what he's about to say even before he says it.

Then something like this happens and I remember there are parts of him I don't understand, that parts of his life are not like the lives of the children around him.

It all started on the day we left the festival in Jerusalem last week. I thought we had lost him forever. We had travelled for a full day before we realised he wasn't with us. I'd been busy packing up and preparing to leave that morning. I'd assumed Jesus was with his cousins—he's always with them.

But I should have checked. I would never have forgiven myself if something had happened. I tried not to panic when we realised he was missing, but as the hours went by and it was clear that no one had seen him all day, I was overwhelmed with fear.

Joseph and I raced back to Jerusalem. The three days that followed were the worst of my life. I truly thought that we had lost our boy.

We searched and searched. We asked so many people if

they'd seen him, but to no avail. I wasn't coping. Thank goodness for Joseph. He held it together for both of us.

Then, on the third day, we looked in the temple. I couldn't believe my eyes when we saw him alive and well. He sat among a group of religious teachers, listening to them and asking them questions.

I sat down on the ground, right there, and cried. Jesus ran over when he saw us. I was angry and asked him how he could have done this to us. He replied with the most peculiar thing. He asked why we'd searched for him—wouldn't we have known he would be in his father's house?

I was shocked into silence. And when the teachers came to speak with us, I saw fascination in their eyes. Jesus amazed them. Their eyes were full of questions about him, but I knew they were questions I couldn't answer. And I still can't.

The teachers were sorry to see him leave. Oh, if I could have been a fly on the wall for the days he'd spent with them.

I don't understand. I know Jesus is special, but he's also my son. I have to keep reminding myself that all I can do is trust God. I look forward to reading through these memories when he is grown. Maybe then I'll have more of an understanding of what God has in store for our boy.

I can hear Joseph and Jesus in their beds now, whispering together about his time with the teachers, and I'm so thankful he's ours.

When Jesus was twelve years old, they attended the festival as usual. After the celebration was over, they started home to Nazareth, but Jesus stayed behind in Jerusalem. His parents didn't miss him at first, because they assumed he was among the other travelers. But when he didn't show up that evening, they started looking for him among their relatives and friends.

When they couldn't find him, they went back to Jerusalem to search for him there. Three days later they finally discovered him in the Temple, sitting among the religious teachers, listening to them and asking questions. All who heard him were amazed at his understanding and his answers.

His parents didn't know what to think. 'Son,' his mother said to him, 'why have you done this to us? Your father and I have been frantic, searching for you everywhere.'

'But why did you need to search?' he asked. 'Didn't you know that I must be in my Father's house?' But they didn't understand what he meant.

Then he returned to Nazareth with them and was obedient to them. And his mother stored all these things in her heart. (Luke 2:42–51)

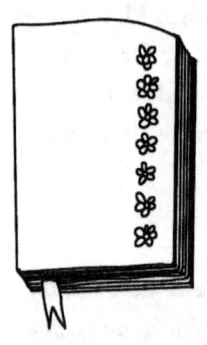

Known

The creator of the universe knows my name.
He has spoken about me.
Sometimes my name is on his lips.

> *The one who formed you says,*
> *'Do not be afraid, for I have ransomed you.*
> *I have called you by name; you are mine.'*
> (Isaiah 43:1)

Hazie

Hazie was the servant of Elisha, the man of God, and Hazie was terrified. When he left the tent this morning, he couldn't believe his eyes. Their tent was completely surrounded by the king of Aram's great army. There were so many chariots and horses surrounding them that Hazie was frozen to the spot, unable to speak. Elisha stepped out of the tent and joined him. Fear overwhelmed Hazie as he looked from one direction to the other.

'Oh, sir, what will we do now?' he whispered. He was pretty sure he knew the answer to that question. They would surely die today.

Hazie knew the king of Aram had been growing more and more upset over his master's ability to hear from the living God. God had warned Elisha many times about the king of Aram's war plans. It seemed God could hear the king speaking even in the privacy of his own bedroom!

Each time God warned Elisha, Elisha warned the Israelite army, who then took the necessary precautions to protect themselves. Elisha always found out about the king's plans. Now it seemed the king of Aram had had enough. He was no doubt here to put a stop to Elisha, and that meant Hazie would die with him. Hazie tried to be brave but trembled with fear as he looked to his master.

Hazie was surprised to see that Elisha wasn't watching the army that surrounded them. Instead, he was looking back at

Hazie, looking calmly into Hazie's eyes. How could he appear so calm at a time like this? They were surely about to meet their end.

'Don't be afraid," Elisha said quietly.

Was he serious? Don't be afraid? Was that all he had to say? Hazie was speechless. His lips moved, but no sound came out.

'There are more on our side than on theirs.' Elisha turned and looked over the hills surrounding them, then looked at the army of Aram, sweeping his eyes from one side of the army to the other.

'O Lord.' Elisha lifted his eyes to the heavens. 'Lord, open his eyes and let him see!' Elisha touched Hazie's shoulder.

Something like scales fell from Hazie's eyes and he gasped. Suddenly they were no longer surrounded by Aram's army alone. Now the hillside was filled with horses and chariots of fire. The magnificence of God's army blazed before them.

Hazie fell to his knees, awestruck at the terrifying sight of the flames of God's army.

When the servant of the man of God got up early the next morning and went outside, there were troops, horses, and chariots everywhere. 'Oh, sir, what will we do now?' the young man cried to Elisha.

'Don't be afraid!' Elisha told him. 'For there are more on our side than on theirs!' Then Elisha prayed, 'O Lord, open his eyes and let him see!' The Lord opened the young man's eyes, and when he looked up, he saw that the hillside around Elisha was filled with horses and chariots of fire. (2 Kings 6:15–17)

Jerusalem

'Lord, see my misery,' Salem cried. 'Look around and see if there is any suffering like mine.' Silence was the reply. Always silence.

Her head pounded. Her tears never ceased to fall down her cheeks. They soaked into her filthy rags.

Salem's majesty and her beauty were stripped away, and she stood naked. Once a warrior, a princess. Now a fallen child.

Salem's needs were unmet, her heart was unloved, her cries were drowned out.

Now she belonged to the enemy.

Now she belonged to the king of Babylon.

Salem had committed a great crime. She had broken the heart of the living God. Betrayed the one who gave her life. He had chosen her and set her apart. Salem's commitment had meant something to him, had meant more than she'd imagined.

Salem's misery was great, and her regret overwhelming.

He had deserted Salem.

Deep down, she understood. A wise parent must punish a child. It wouldn't be love to let a child roam free. Guidelines were a necessity, obedience a virtue. How much more must the creator know this to be true? And so he punished her, his treasure.

Salem had lost it all—her home, family, security, treasures, riches, her beauty. All her glory was gone.

Was there a plan? Did the creator understand that Salem couldn't rid herself of her sinful condition? No matter how much she tried, her stains would find her.

Salem needed a saviour. There was no other way. She needed someone strong enough to hold her heavy burdens, to own her punishment, to wipe her slate clean. She didn't deserve it, but her need was evident.

Did the creator have a plan? Did he have a hero in mind? Would he send his son for her?

Jerusalem, once so full of people, is now deserted.
She sobs through the night; tears stream down her cheeks.
Judah has been led away into captivity, oppressed with
cruel slavery.
All the majesty of beautiful Jerusalem has been
stripped away.
Jerusalem has sinned greatly, so she has been tossed away
like a filthy rag.
She defiled herself with immorality and gave no thought
to her future.
'Lord, see my misery,' she cries. 'The enemy has
triumphed.'
The enemy has plundered her completely, taking every
precious thing she owns.
'Look around and see if there is any suffering like mine'.
(Lamentations 1:1–3, 6, 8–10, 12)

Surrendered

He had never been so hungry before. Never. But he had never been so full either. And no amount of belly rumbling or hunger pain could drown out the Spirit that bubbled up within him. The Spirit left him feeling fuller than he had ever felt. The hunger pains reminded him of his baptism, which brought him joy. The hunger pains were consistent and a perfect reminder. That was the moment the Holy Spirit had come upon him so heavily that Jesus would never be the same. It was surreal, it was tangible. His stomach growled and he held out his open palms to the heavens, joyful tears pricking the corner of his eyes. He'd lost count of how many days it had been, but it was incredible how long he was able to go without food.

It had begun—his ministry—and he was hungry for it.

Then Jesus was led by the Spirit into the wilderness to be tempted there by the devil. For forty days and forty nights he fasted and became very hungry. (Matthew 4:1–2)

Evi

Evi was an Israelite girl who had been taken from Israel and placed in a home in Aram to serve as a maid to the mistress of the house, Prisy. Although Prisy was kind, Evi had struggled terribly at first with what had become of her life. It had been a couple of years now, and Evi had adjusted to her new position and her new home. She had grown close to Prisy and was surprisingly happy. Evi was even able to speak openly and freely when alone with her mistress. Prisy had become almost like a mother figure.

Evi was folding Prisy's clothing into neat piles onto her bed as her mistress dressed and put on her makeup behind her. Prisy was getting ready for an evening out with her husband, Naaman. Naaman was a good man, and Evi had grown fond of him as well. Though she missed her own family terribly, Evi thanked God every night that he had protected her, and placed her with a kind family.

Naaman entered her mistress's room, and Evi stood to attention. Naaman greeted Evi with a smile then kissed his wife on the cheek. Naaman winced slightly as he straightened, and Evi averted her eyes, focusing back to her washing pile. Her master was sick. Evi knew about it, and she knew how much her mistress worried for him. Naaman had leprosy. It wasn't too bad—yet. He was still able to work. He had a very important job. As far as Evi could gather, he was the commander of the king's army.

'How long will you be, honey?' he asked quietly.

'Almost ready.' Prisy puckered her lips before the mirror and lathered on her lipstick while Evi added to her pile of laundry.

'I'll be downstairs,' Namaan said as he left the room.

Evi's heart beat hard against her chest. She'd wanted to speak to Prisy about this for a while now, but had made excuse after excuse as to why she shouldn't. Perhaps now would be a good time. She glanced at her mistress, who was straightening her dress in front of the mirror.

'Madam,' Evi said quietly, so quietly it was almost a whisper. But Prisy heard her.

'Yes, Evi.' Prisy didn't turn to face her. Instead, she reached for her bag and filled it with items from her dresser.

Evi cleared her throat. Why was she so nervous?

'I wish my master would go to see the prophet in Samaria,' Evi said. There. She'd said it.

Prisy turned to look at her, her expression puzzled.

'What do you mean?' Prisy asked.

Evi had Prisy's full attention now and it made her even more nervous, but she had begun, so she must finish. Evi took a deep breath and went on.

'I wish he would go to see the prophet in Samaria, because the prophet would heal him of his leprosy.'

Prisy sat on her bed and patted a space beside her, asking Evi to join her.

'Have you seen this prophet you speak of perform such healings before?' Prisy asked, her eyes alight with hope.

Evi nodded. When she was a very young child, she had seen him heal a woman who was covered in leprosy much worse than that of her master, and the woman had been completely restored. Evi would never forget something like that.

They were out late that night, and Evi wondered if her mistress had told Naaman about the prophet, but she couldn't ask. It wasn't until the following evening when Naaman did not return home from work that Evi realised he had taken a trip. Later, after supper, her mistress pulled her aside and let her know Naaman had gone to see the prophet in Israel.

Evi felt sick to her stomach, like there were millions of butterflies flying around in there. She escaped to her room as soon as she could, got down on her knees beside her bed and prayed to God for Naaman. She prayed God's prophet would heal Naaman and her master would be well.

The following night, Evi was woken by the sound of screaming from the downstairs room. Evi sat up in bed, heart hammering as she listened to the muffled sounds coming through her floorboards. Was there something wrong? No—it sounded like rejoicing. Evi swung her legs from her bed and crept down the stairs, where she stood out of sight beside the door and listened.

'Is it gone? All of it?' That was Prisy's voice. Evi's heart skipped a beat.

'It's gone,' Namaan replied. 'My skin is as good as new.' His voice cracked, and Evi's eyes filled with tears. She should leave. She was eavesdropping, but her feet stayed where they were.

'The prophet didn't even come from his home to see me,' Naaman said. 'He had his servant tell me to go and wash in the river seven times. I was furious that he wouldn't face me. I started home, refusing to do as he said.' Naaman paused. 'Thank goodness I changed my mind.' The passion in his voice was evident.

There was silence.

'I love you,' Prisy whispered through her sobs.

'I know now there is no other God in all the world except for the God of Israel,' Naaman said quietly.

Evi couldn't believe her ears. Tears fell down her cheeks as she silently tiptoed back up the stairs to her bedroom.

At this time Aramean raiders had invaded the land of Israel, and among their captives was a young girl who had been given to Naaman's wife as a maid. One day the girl said to her mistress, 'I wish my master would go to see the prophet in Samaria. He would heal him of his leprosy.' (2 Kings 5:2–3)

Designer

They had disobeyed him and would have to leave now.
He sat in the garden. Taking materials from those he had
created, he made them clothing with his own hands.
He knew their sizes well, their exact dimensions.
He made them different, one for her and one for him.

*And the Lord God made clothing from animal skins for
Adam and his wife.* (Genesis 3:21)

Leftovers

There was a piece of broiled fish left over from dinner. Luke knew Jesus liked broiled fish, but even as Luke reached for it, his hands shook, and his mind reeled. Luke handed the fish to Jesus and drew back to stand with his friends, their faces as pale as his own.

They watched as Jesus kneeled to sit beside the table. They had all watched him eat dinner countless times. But they had never watched the way they did tonight. Jesus held the fish in his left hand and used his right to peel a mouthful away. He moved fast—he was hungry. He swallowed his first mouthful while preparing his second, pulling at the fish until a piece broke free. As he lifted the fish to his mouth, the nail wound was plain to see.

Luke swallowed over the lump forming in his throat. Strands of Jesus' dark hair fell over the side of his face and he used the back of his hand to push them away. Luke had seen him do the same thing too many times to count—it was him. He was here. Their friend, their Saviour, their Lord. He had been dead, and now he sat in the house before them eating broiled fish.

Jesus had almost finished the fish, and his strength looked to be returning. He looked up at Luke and the others as he chewed his last mouthful, then wiped his hands. He smiled a slight smile, and his eyes shone with love for his friends, a look Luke had become accustomed to but had never expected to see again. They were in shock—Luke had never heard the rowdy bunch so quiet.

'When I was with you before, I told you that everything written about me in the law of Moses and the prophets and in the psalms must be fulfilled,' Jesus said quietly.

Luke felt peace fall over him, almost as though a substance had fallen over his mind. He was sure the others experienced it too. Luke drew closer to Jesus and took the seat beside him. The others relaxed into the room and listened.

'It was written long ago that the Messiah would suffer and die and rise from the dead on the third day. It was also written that this message would be proclaimed in the authority of his name to all the nations, beginning in Jerusalem: "There is forgiveness of sins for all who repent".'

Luke held his breath, the wonder of what Jesus' death meant for humanity settling over his spirit. Now there was forgiveness for sins? Now no more animal sacrifices needed to be made? Was Jesus' sacrifice the end of striving for forgiveness?

Jesus watched their faces, quietly taking in the room. 'You are witnesses of all these things,' he told them.

Now Luke understood.

'Why are you frightened?' he asked. 'Why are your hearts filled with doubt? Look at my hands. Look at my feet. You can see that it's really me. Touch me and make sure that I am not a ghost, because ghosts don't have bodies, as you see that I do.' As he spoke, he showed them his hands and his feet.

Still they stood there in disbelief, filled with joy and

wonder. Then he asked them, 'Do you have anything here to eat?' They gave him a piece of broiled fish, and he ate it as they watched. (Luke 24:38–43)

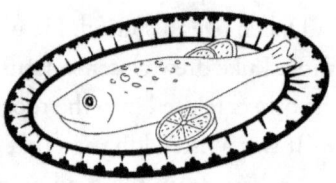

Winnie

Early morning mist covered the mountain and there was no one in sight.

Winnie clung to her harp and used the other hand to push a tree branch aside. She climbed, the leaves and early morning dew crunching beneath her shoes.

The path led around the mountain, becoming steeper as Winnie went on. Daylight touched the edge of the night, and the mist made it hard to see. Still Winnie's feet continued on. Did they know where his hidden path lay? *Or were they led by his truth and his light?*

The sound of Winnie's breath and the crunch beneath her shoes were the only sounds in the stillness of the morning.

Her anticipation rose.

'Could this be the place that you live?' Winnie whispered.

Send out your light and your truth; let them guide me. Let them lead me to your holy mountain, to the place where you live.

There I will go to the altar of God, to God—the source of all my joy. I will praise you with my harp, O God, my God! (Psalm 43:3–4)

Japha

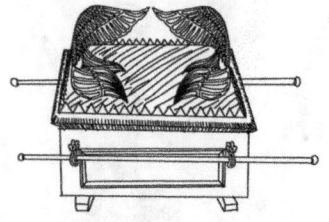

Japha had worshipped the god Dagon since he was a young child. He had always been loyal to Dagon and he always would be. Today Dagon had won Japha and his people a victory unlike any other! They had defeated the Israelite army. As Japha travelled home, he praised and worshipped Dagon with all his heart. Dagon had never come through for his people quite like this before, and Japha was astounded at his power. For the longest of times, the Israelites had been undefeated. It was true—their God was powerful! But not as powerful as Dagon. Japha smirked to himself as he directed his donkey down toward his road. He was almost home.

Perhaps the most miraculous part of their victory wasn't that they had defeated the Israelite army and sent them running, but they had somehow managed to capture the ark of the Israelite God. They had captured it and brought it home with them. Japha heard the ark had been placed inside Dagon's glorious temple and now it sat beside the idol of Dagon himself.

They had been victorious and Japha was full of pride as he fell asleep that night. First thing in the morning, he would go to the temple to worship Dagon and to see the captured ark of Israel's God.

Japha rose early, sure he'd never felt so excited to visit Dagon's temple. He dressed and made his bed, ate quickly, fetched some water, then made his way into town. He was so early that most people had not yet risen, and the town was quiet.

Japha was pleased. He wanted to pour out his thanks and praise to Dagon and preferred to pray in private, at least to begin with. He rode straight to the temple, where he tied his donkey close to the entrance. He took the stairs two at a time and peeled open the door, stepping in quietly, and closing the door behind him before turning to face the statue of Dagon.

But what he saw caused him to jump backwards and hit his head on the closed door behind him. He held his hand over where he'd struck the door. He was speechless, in utter shock.

What had happened here? How could this be?

The glorious statue of Dagon was lying face down before the ark of Israel's God. Dagon's face touched the floor before the ark as though he were worshipping the God of Israel.

Who could have done this? Who could be strong enough to move Dagon's statue?

Japha didn't know, but he turned away in anguish, swung the door open and ran from the temple to sound the alarm.

After the Philistines captured the Ark of God, they took it from the battleground at Ebenezer to the town of Ashdod. They carried the Ark of God into the temple of Dagon and placed it beside an idol of Dagon. But when the citizens of Ashdod went to see it the next morning, Dagon had fallen with his face to the ground in front of the Ark of the Lord!
(1 Samuel 5:1–3)

Listen

He paused, stopped, and bent down.
Why did the creator of the universe bend down so low?
Why did he stop in his tracks and stoop to the ground?

> *Because he bends down to listen, I will pray as long as
> I have breath.* (Psalm 116:2)

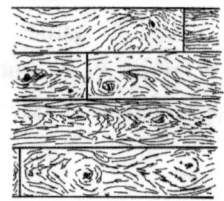

Rebeka

Rebeka changed into her nightwear, sighing as she sat down heavily on her bed. It had been another ordinary day and Rebeka was bored. Rebeka had always been obedient to her parents and was careful to live her life close to God. But as much as she loved both her home and her family, if she was honest with herself, she ached to leave them. And it wasn't that anything was wrong with her home. Rebeka's parents were kind and devoted to her. They had given her a childhood filled with love and taught her how to live life in a respectful way.

But for as long as she could remember, Rebeka had longed to explore! She wanted to see beyond the confines of her community. There had to be more out there. Some days she felt it calling to her. She yearned to be a part of something bigger than she could see. Rebeka wanted to travel, she wanted romance, she wanted to feel alive.

Rebeka had never been in love. There had been a shepherd boy named Zaith who moved to the area when Rebeka was twelve, but he hadn't stayed long and had been too shy to reply to Rebeka's morning greetings on her way to the well. Besides, her parents wouldn't allow a suitor unless it was somebody they approved of. Rebeka worried that she might never find anybody suitable, that she would be alone forever. She lay in her bed in the dark, staring at her bedroom roof. She sighed again and turned over to wrap her arms around her pillow, snuggling down with her face close to the wall.

'Would you let my life begin?' Rebeka whispered to him. It was the same prayer every night. 'Would you do what only you can do, Lord, and satisfy the deep longings of my heart?' With that, Rebeka closed her eyes and a peace fell over her as she drifted off to sleep. She was sure she could trust him with it.

***

The next day, Rebeka held her water jug on her shoulder as she headed to the spring out of town to collect water. It had been a hot day, so Rebeka had waited until evening to come. The other women had the same idea. Although Rebeka had a head start, she could hear them behind her.

As Rebeka approached the spring, she noticed a man standing off to the side. Camels rested beside him, and he was watching her. Rebeka smiled at the stranger. He nodded in response. He looked nervous.

She lowered her jug from her shoulder and filled it with water, wondering about the stranger. Where had he come from? The jug was much heavier once filled, but Rebeka was strong, having collected water for many years now. She made her way up the path from the spring, heading back towards the town gate. Suddenly, the strange man with the camels ran to meet her.

'Please, can you give me a drink of water from your jug?' he asked.

'Of course.' Rebeka lowered her jug from her shoulder and let him drink. She glanced behind him at his camels.

'I'll draw water for your camels too, until they have had enough to drink.' The stranger didn't reply. Instead, he froze, staring at Rebeka, as though he'd seen a ghost. Odd. Though he did not reply, Rebeka guessed he didn't mind—after all, the camels would be thirsty. So she ran back down to fill up her jug.

Rebeka stood beside the camels as they drank, wanting to make sure she'd drawn enough. The stranger approached her and pulled a gold earring and two gold bracelets from his bag. He handed them to Rebeka. Rebeka was sure she had never seen such beautiful jewellery. But why was he giving these to her? She had only offered him water. Rebeka opened her mouth to speak, but words escaped her.

'Whose daughter are you?' the stranger asked. 'And please tell me, would your father have room to put us up for the night?'

'I am the daughter of Bethuel,' she replied, but didn't take her eyes from the delicate gold bracelet on her wrist. 'My grandparents are Nahor and Milcah, and yes, we have room for guests.'

That evening, as Rebeka prepared for dinner, she admired her new jewellery before heading down the stairs. The generous stranger would join them for dinner, and Rebeka was eager to hear his story.

As Rebeka made her way down the stairs, she could hear her family in the dining room.

'I don't want to eat until I have told you why I have come.' That was the stranger's voice. Rebeka stopped on the last step before entering the dining room and listened.

'All right, then. Tell us.' Rebeka's brother replied.

'I am Abraham's servant,' the stranger said. Abraham was Rebeka's uncle. Amazing!

'The Lord has greatly blessed my master, and he has become a very wealthy man,' the stranger continued. 'My master has a son, and he has given his son everything he owns. But my master made me take an oath. He said, "Do not allow my son to marry one of these local Canaanite women. Instead, go to my father's house, to my relatives, and find a wife there for my son.""

As the stranger spoke, Rebeka felt as though the world had slowed right down, and the blood rushed from her face. She reached out and held onto the wall beside the stairs, slowly lowering herself to sit on the bottom step.

'Today when I came to the spring, I prayed this prayer: "O, Lord God of my master, Abraham, please give me success on this mission. See, I am standing here beside this spring. This is my request. When a young woman comes to draw water, I will say to her, 'Please give me a little drink of water from your jug.' If she says, 'Yes, have a drink, and I will draw water for your camels too,' then let her be the one you have selected to be the wife of my master's son.""

Rebeka's spirit felt like it was on fire as she listened to his words. Had God heard her prayers? Was something happening that could change everything for Rebeka? Was her life about to begin? Even as the questions formed in her mind, the stirring in her spirit whispered to her, *It is time.*

'I had not even finished praying in my heart when I saw Rebeka coming out with her water jug,' the servant said. 'And when I asked her who her parents were, I realised God had sent me straight to my master's relatives.'

Rebeka couldn't sleep that night. She tossed and turned in a mixture of excitement and nerves at the prospect of how her life had changed in one moment. She rose early the following morning and heard her parents calling for her. When she got downstairs, she was surprised to see Abraham's servant was already up and speaking with her parents.

Rebeka's mother was crying. What was going on? She kissed Rebeka on the forehead and told her to sit down.

'We were hoping you would stay for a couple of weeks so we could say goodbye to you properly,' her mother said. 'But Abraham's servant wants to leave today.' Rebeka could hear the anguish in her mother's voice, and her own heartbeat pounding against her ears. She waited for it.

'Are you willing to go with this man?' her mother asked. There it was. The question Rebeka had been waiting for since before she could remember.

'Yes, I will go,' Rebeka replied with no hesitation. Rebeka would miss her family and felt for her mother, but God had heard her prayers.

Her own life was about to begin.

Before he had finished praying, he saw a young woman named Rebekah coming out with her water jug on her shoulder. She was the daughter of Bethuel, who was the son of Abraham's brother Nahor and his wife, Milcah.

The servant watched her in silence, wondering whether or not the Lord had given him success in his mission. Then at last, when the camels had finished drinking, he took out a gold ring for her nose and two large gold bracelets for her wrists.

'But we want Rebekah to stay with us at least ten days,' her brother and mother said. 'Then she can go.'

'Well,' they said, 'we'll call Rebekah and ask her what she thinks.' So they called Rebekah. 'Are you willing to go with this man?' they asked her. And she replied, 'Yes, I will go.' (Genesis 24:15, 21–22, 55, 57–58)

When my heart began to beat – you watched me.

You watched me as I was being formed in utter seclusion,
as I was woven together in the dark of the womb.
(Psalm 139:15)

Roo

They were heading back to Tarshish, and Roo was pleased to be going home. He had missed Esli and the kids more than usual on this trip, and it would be good to sleep in his own bed.

It was time for the ship to leave, and Roo was growing impatient with the unending line of passengers. Roo was responsible for handing out tickets. He tried to keep a cheerful disposition as he dealt with the passengers, but grew more and more restless, eager to be on his way. Finally he greeted the last customer in line, a young man who seemed nervous as he glanced back over his shoulder.

'Hello there.' Roo greeted the stranger. The man simply nodded and handed over his payment. Roo observed him curiously as he reached for his ticket.

'What brings you aboard today?' Roo asked the odd fellow. It was a nosy question, but something about the man had caught his attention and he was interested.

The stranger looked at Roo for the first time, shuffling from one foot to the other. Roo had been right. There was something peculiar about him. Odd as he seemed, nothing could have prepared Roo for his response.

'I'm running away from the Lord,' he said quietly. With that, he put his head down and shuffled on past, following the other passengers downstairs to the hold below. Roo watched the back of him until he was out of sight. When he realised that his mouth was hanging open, he shook his head and pulled down the barrier.

They set off on their journey. Roo went about his duties, his mind wandering back and forth between the odd man down below and Esli. He couldn't wait to be home. Night was approaching, and the passengers would soon be asleep. The night was calm, and it looked like they would have a smooth journey. Roo went below to ensure the passengers had all they needed. He spotted the strange man from earlier, already in his bunk.

Roo headed back to the deck, taking the steps two at a time. A strong gust came out of nowhere, and the ship shuddered to the side. Roo missed the step he'd been aiming for, tripped but managed to land on his wrists, his face just inches from the steps.

What in the world was that?

Roo arrived on deck to see his fellow sailors pointing out across the ocean. What had been a crystal-clear night, had become a hazardous-looking storm in a matter of minutes. It was approaching fast. Roo held the rail as another gust of wind took hold of the ship.

The next hour passed in a blur. Roo had never experienced a storm so sudden that no one had seen it coming. There was hollering and panic as the crew battled against the waves, which seemed to grow in size by the minute.

'Abort the cargo!' Captain Boz shouted.

Roo could hardly believe his ears. In all his years working for Boz, he had never expected to hear those words come from his boss's mouth. But obeying the captain was easier said than done. Roo and the rest of the crew were thrown relentlessly against the side of the ship as they tried to toss the cargo overboard.

Still the storm raged. Roo feared for his life. Would he ever see Esli again? Would he see his children? The thought sickened him, and he wiped the sea water from his eyes as the wind howled through his ears.

'The ship can't take this much longer. It could break apart.' Boz called to the crew. 'Pray to your gods.' Boz dropped to his knees beside the rail, and bowed his head.

Suddenly the strange man's face from earlier flashed before Roo's eyes and he recalled his words. *I am running away from the Lord.* The blood drained from his face as he realised the significance of the man's words.

He repeated the words to Boz as the wind howled around them. Boz bolted for the stairs. Roo followed him, crashing into the railing as he went.

The passengers were huddled together in a corner, but the strange man was still sleeping. Unbelievable. Boz shook the man awake. The stranger sat up, gripping the blanket, his eyes wide and fearful.

'How can you sleep at a time like this? Get up and pray to your God! Maybe he will pay attention to us and spare our lives.'

The man looked like he would be sick as he stood to his feet and followed them out. They found the crew casting lots, desperate and trying to figure out why the storm had ravaged their ship. Roo, Boz, and the stranger were passed a sheep knuckle. They cast their lots, revealing the stranger was to blame for the storm.

'Why has this violent storm come down on us?'

'Who are you?' Boz asked.

'What is your line of work?' Members of the crew fired their questions at him.

'What country are you from?'

'What is your nationality?'

The man's face crumbled, and he dropped his head into his hands before looking up again at Roo and the crew.

'I am Jonah, a Hebrew.' He paused 'I worship the Lord, the God of heaven, who made the sea and the land.'

Roo didn't know who he spoke of, but Jonah's words knocked the breath out of him. He looked at Boz, the fear in his eyes mirroring his own.

'Why are you running from your God?' Roo asked.

Jonah relayed his story. God had asked him to go somewhere to deliver a message, and Jonah hadn't wanted to. He had boarded their ship instead. He had put all of their lives in danger. The crew were thrown to the floor of the ship as a giant wave knocked into them, filling their ship with water. Roo hit his head, and groaned.

'Jonah, why did you do it?' he yelled.

'What should we do to you to make it stop?' Boz took control.

'Throw me into the sea and it will become calm again. I know this terrible storm is my fault!' Jonah shouted.

Roo was tempted. He wanted to see his family, he didn't want to die for this man's sins, but Boz wouldn't have it. They tried harder, rowing with all their strength, fighting against the storm. But the storm only became angrier.

Roo watched Boz's face. Roo could tell he was battling, but the decision lay with him. Finally he stopped rowing and lifted his head to the skies.

'O Lord.' Boz glanced down at Jonah, as if to check he had addressed Jonah's God correctly.

Jonah nodded.

'Don't make us die for this man's sin,' Boz called into the

wind. He closed his eyes and massaged his temples, one hand holding the rail. 'Don't hold us responsible for his death.'

With that, Boz nodded at his crew. Roo froze, his hands clenching the oar, as two of their largest crew members lifted Jonah, carried him to the side, and threw him overboard. Roo leant over the rail and watched until Jonah disappeared beneath the raging seas.

The wind stopped.

The water calmed and the ship stood almost completely still.

There was silence aboard the boat. Roo didn't know what to think. Relief rushed through his body and he kept his eyes on the water in search of Jonah, but he was gone.

But Jonah got up and went in the opposite direction to get away from the Lord. He went down to the port of Joppa, where he found a ship leaving for Tarshish. He bought a ticket and went on board, hoping to escape from the Lord by sailing to Tarshish.

Now the Lord had arranged for a great fish to swallow Jonah. And Jonah was inside the fish for three days and three nights. (Jonah 1:3, 17)

Remembered

He opened his hands, revealing his palms.
Palms large and capable, strong and steady.
Bare but for a name.
My name.

> *I would not forget you! See, I have written your name on
> the palms of my hands.* (Isaiah 49:15–16)

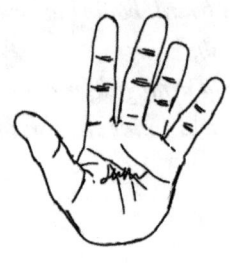

Hush

Hush was a large stone who lived beside the road, next to a terebinth tree in the land of Shechem. Hush knew he was just a stone, but he longed for more. He wanted more than his life had offered him. Hush had sat in the same spot for many years.

On the odd occasion, a child travelling with their family had stumbled upon Hush, climbed up onto his large body and jumped back down to the ground below. Those days were few and far between, but they were among the most special moments of Hush's life. Yet he longed for more.

Was this deep longing within him common among the other stones, or had it been placed within him alone? Had Hush been created with a purpose? Or would he always be nothing more than a large stone sitting beside the road, lonely and bored? He thought about it often. He spoke to the creator about it often. Then he sat and he waited.

One day, something happened, right next to where Hush sat beside the road. Joshua, the leader of the Israelites, and all the Israelite tribes gathered together. Everyone, including their elders, leaders, judges, and officers. They were close enough that Hush could hear their every word. How exhilarating! Hush listened intently to the unfolding conversation.

Joshua addressed the gathered crowd.

'Don't you remember?' he called out to them.

The passion in his voice was evident, and Hush wondered if he might cry.

'Don't you remember that it was our God who rescued us from slavery in Egypt? God wants you to remember it was he who parted the sea so our ancestors could walk straight through.'

It sounded to Hush like the people may have forgotten something important. Had the Israelites forgotten about their rescuer? Had they forgotten that the creator of the universe had freed their nation? Astounded, Hush listened as Joshua continued.

'Don't you remember it was our God who brought us into this land, the land he promised us? This land we call home, this land that flows with milk and honey. It was God who fought our enemies for us so we would obtain this promised land.'

Hush was sure now—Joshua was definitely crying. Hush hung on his every word, knowing he would not forget a single detail for as long as time remained.

'So who do you choose?' Joshua asked the crowd. 'Will you choose to serve the Lord your God? Or will you choose to serve other gods—gods who don't even exist, gods who were created by human hands from gold and silver?'

Hush held his breath. Who would the Israelites choose? Was there even a choice? Hush didn't think so but he listened and he waited.

'We would never abandon the Lord and serve other gods,' the people shouted. Phew! That was a relief.

Joshua stood silently for a long time, looking intently at the Israelites. Did he believe them? Hush couldn't be sure.

'So you have chosen to serve the Lord?' he finally asked.

'Yes, we will serve the Lord our God. We will obey only him,' the people replied.

Joshua nodded, then he walked the short distance

between himself and Hush. Hush held his breath as Joshua placed his arms around Hush's large body. Joshua pushed and heaved Hush, pulling him until Hush was standing beside him, beneath the terebinth tree beside the tabernacle of the Lord. Hush had looked at the tree his entire life and had never dreamed he would ever sit beneath its shade. Yet here he was.

Joshua still had one hand on Hush as he turned back to face the crowd.

'This stone has heard everything the Lord said to us.'

Hush could hardly believe his ears … but Joshua was right. He had heard every word. How had Joshua known?

'It will be a witness to testify against you if you go back on your word to God,' Joshua said. All of the people looked at Hush.

A witness! Hush played the word over and over again. He felt like all his wildest dreams had come true.

He was a witness.

As a reminder of their agreement, he took a huge stone and rolled it beneath the terebinth tree beside the Tabernacle of the Lord.

Joshua said to all the people, 'This stone has heard everything the Lord said to us. It will be a witness to testify against you if you go back on your word to God.' (Joshua 24:26–27)

The Kiss

It was a simple kiss, but it had the power to change everything.

It was a planned kiss, unlike the peck of a greeting or an unexpected introduction. A plan predicted not just by the one who betrayed, but by a prophet long ago. It was not a kiss of love or friendship, but of greed and betrayal.

The kiss left his lips, arriving at its destination—on the cheek of a hero, one who chose to receive it.

Where a kiss may bring life, hope and promise, this kiss delivered prosecution, fear and darkness. A kiss of death.

He who delivered the kiss was deceived, blinded by his love for money. The receiver's eyes were wide open, blinded only by his love for his father and for humanity.

The traitor's lips were puckered as he leaned in close. He pressed his pursed lips into the cheek of Jesus. A familiar cheek, a familiar scent—his breath, his eyes, his facial hair, all familiar. He had loved Jesus and now he killed him with his kiss.

The traitor, Judas, had given them a prearranged signal: 'You will know which one to arrest when I greet him with a kiss. Then you can take him away under guard.' As soon as they arrived, Judas walked up to Jesus. 'Rabbi!' he exclaimed, and gave him the kiss. (Mark 14:44–45)

Mela

Mela sat at the water's edge and dangled her feet into the river. It was her third day in a row at the Jordan River. Mela's home was in the desert, so she was able to run down on her own.

There was something exciting happening at the river. A man named John had been there for weeks, and crowds of people were coming to listen to him. Mela was over the moon! She'd never seen so many people close to her home.

She didn't understand most of what John said. But she could feel his words, like they were burning in her chest. Strange.

John's speaking was exciting. He made it sound as if something was coming, as if something big was on its way. She wanted to know what. It was part of the reason she kept coming back to the river.

The water felt cool between her toes, but her eyes were on John. He was the most interesting man Mela had ever seen. He wore a leather belt and unusual clothing made of camel's hair. His hands were rough and Mela got the feeling he slept outside.

John bent down to wash his hands in the river, then stood up to face the crowd. He closed his eyes, as though in deep concentration.

'There is someone coming after me,' John called out to the crowd. His eyes opened wide, and Mela sat up straight. She would try to get a clue today. She would concentrate as hard as she could and try to find out more about who might be coming.

'He is the one who comes after me,' John continued. 'And though his ministry follows mine, I'm not even worthy to be his slave or untie the straps of his sandals.'

John seemed so capable, so who could he be speaking about? Who could be coming that John couldn't even serve?

John stepped further into the river. His skin was brown from the sun and his hair was much longer than Mela's. She knew what he would do now. He would baptise the people.

'Come to me, repent of your sins,' he called out. 'I will baptise you today with water, but the one who is coming is mightier than I, and he will baptise you with the Holy Spirit and with fire!'

Mela's heart pounded against her chest. Some people stepped down into the water. Every day more people were baptised. Mela had felt too shy to step down into the water, even though she wanted to.

A man sat down beside Mela, and dipped his feet into the river.

'Hi, Mela,' he greeted her. How did he know her name? Was he a friend of her father?

'Hello,' she replied.

'Are you going to be baptised today?' the stranger asked, as though reading her mind.

'I'm thinking about it,' Mela admitted. 'Are you going to be baptised?'

The stranger looked out over the water as John dipped a young man beneath the surface. Mela watched the stranger's face and wondered if he might be nervous too. It was obvious he wanted to be baptised by the way he watched John so intently. She felt sorry for him.

'I will if you will.' It was a brave suggestion, and she instantly regretted her words.

He didn't answer, but instead smiled down at her. She took that as a yes. The friendly man stepped into the water and waded out to where John stood. It seemed he was going first.

John pulled another young woman up from the water and sent her off to the shore, then turned his attention toward Mela's new friend.

John froze, staring at the stranger, and his mouth hung open. Did they know one another? Mela couldn't figure it out. Why did John look so alarmed? John raised both his hands and held them on top of his head. He shook his head as he looked at the stranger.

'I am the one who needs to be baptised by you,' John said. 'So why are you coming to me?'

Wait. What was going on here? The crowd was silent, all eyes on the conversation unfolding in the river.

'It should be done this way,' the stranger replied, 'for we must carry out all that God requires.'

Mela held her breath and strained her ears to hear. All that God requires? What did he mean?

John was quiet, watching the stranger, as though he was trying to come to terms with these events.

'Very well,' John said. He took the stranger's hand and proceeded to dunk him under the water. All the while, tears ran down John's cheeks. Why was he upset?

John lifted the stranger from the water. When they stood, the clouds parted, and light shone down around them. The light was so bright that Mela shielded her eyes.

Then something seemed to fall onto the stranger. Mela couldn't see what it was, but it floated down like a dove and settled on his head.

'What was that?' a woman near Mela whispered. There were gasps and hushed whispers.

Mela realised she'd been holding her breath and slowly exhaled. Was it possible this stranger was the one who John had been speaking about? Could the stranger be the one John said was coming after him?

Mela couldn't be sure, but she got the feeling that whoever this man was, he would have got baptised today regardless of their deal.

'This is my son.' The voice was loud and clear, but where had it come from? Mela spun around, looking to the left and the right.

'My son whom I love; and who brings me great joy.' The voice spoke again. It seemed to come from everywhere, from way up high and from right in close beside Mela's ear. But she still couldn't see who was speaking.

This is the good news about Jesus the Messiah, the Son of God. It began just as the prophet Isaiah had written:

'Look, I am sending my messenger ahead of you, and he will prepare your way. He is a voice shouting in the wilderness, "Prepare the way for the Lord's coming! Clear the road for him!"'

This messenger was John the Baptist. He was in the wilderness and preached that people should be baptised to show that they had turned to God to be forgiven. All of Judea, including all the people of Jerusalem, went out to see and hear John.

John announced: 'Someone is coming soon who is greater than I am—so much greater that I'm not even worthy to stoop down like a slave and untie the straps of his sandals. I baptise you with water, but he will baptise you with the Holy Spirit!'

One day Jesus came from Nazareth in Galilee, and John baptised him in the Jordan River. As Jesus came up out of the water, he saw the heavens splitting apart and the Holy Spirit descending on him like a dove. And a voice from heaven said, 'You are my dearly loved Son, and you bring me great joy.' (Mark 1:1–5, 7–11)

Alive

He breathed, filling his lungs with air. The fabric close to his nose rose and fell with each new breath. He opened his eyes. His eyelashes brushed the fabric. It was white, all white. His arms were strapped down at his sides and his legs were held firmly together.

He was alive. It was done. It was over.

Those with him unwrapped the fabric that held him until he stood free beside his resting place. He took the cloth that had wrapped his head and folded it. His work here was done. A tear rolled down his face as he placed it down, separate from the other strips of linen.

Then he walked from the tomb.

Peter and the other disciple started out for the tomb. They were both running, but the other disciple outran Peter and reached the tomb first.

He stooped and looked in and saw the linen wrappings lying there, but he didn't go in.

Then Simon Peter arrived and went inside. He also noticed the linen wrappings lying there, while the cloth that had covered Jesus' head was folded up and lying apart from the other wrappings.

Then the disciple who had reached the tomb first also went in, and he saw and believed—for until then they still hadn't understood the Scriptures that said Jesus must rise from the dead. (John 20:3–9)

Remy

Remy was a teacher of religious law, and a fine one at that. He had surpassed his peers in their studies, and had gone on to make a name for himself as one of the leading teachers in Jerusalem. And this was why he couldn't move. This was why it felt like the breath had been clear knocked from his lungs.

Remy stood with his friends at the foot of the crosses, all teachers and leaders. As they chatted and conversed around him, Remy stood, feet planted on the grass, unable to move.

The criminal nailed to the middle cross was named Jesus, and Remy had helped to put him there. He had seen to it, used every power of persuasion he could muster, and they had succeeded in their plot. He should have been pleased. And he had been pleased … until Jesus spoke from the cross. The words he called out sent a shiver up Remy's spine, not because of their meaning but because Remy knew the scripture too well. He knew it word for word. The words came back to him now, one after another. Time slowed down, and Remy found it hard to breathe.

Someone grabbed him by the arm.

'Is everything all right, Remy?' Macah asked. 'You look like you've seen a ghost.'

Remy gulped and forced a smile. *Breathe. Remember to breathe.*

'Yes. All is well.' He turned his attention back to the crosses before them.

'He deserves everything that has come to him.' Macah shook his head, and Remy knew he spoke of Jesus.

Remy nodded. It was all that he could do, although he wasn't sure he still agreed. He didn't know what to think.

'Did you hear what he called out?' Macah asked. Remy couldn't speak, and Macah took that as a sign he hadn't heard. 'He called "My God, my God, why have you abandoned me?"' Macah raised his eyebrows at Remy. 'You know what that means?'

Remy shook his head.

'No,' although he was afraid he did.

'I guess he's finally accepted God is not with him. Unfortunately it's a little too late.' Macah chuckled, and turned away from Remy to talk to the person on his other side.

Remy knew too much. In particular, he knew the ancient scriptures. The words Jesus called out to God weren't new to Remy. They were written in the scriptures by King David himself, thousands of years before. But it wasn't Jesus' words that shook Remy. It was that Remy knew the next words in the scriptures. They ran through his mind now, one after another.

Everyone who sees me mocks me,
they sneer and shake their heads.
Let the Lord save him, if the Lord loves him so much.
My life is poured out like water,
and all my bones are out of joint.
My heart is like wax melting within me.
My strength has dried up like sunbaked clay.
My tongue sticks to the roof of my mouth.
They have pierced my hands and feet.

*They divide my garments among themselves
and throw dice for my clothing.*

Something like scales fell from Remy's eyes. It was as though he could clearly see for the first time that the scriptures he held so dear to his heart, the scriptures he had memorised as a young child … did they speak of this man?

He lifted his head to the cross where Jesus hung. Did the scriptures speak of Jesus? The question was like a heavy noose around his neck and Remy's heart felt as though it might burst from his chest.

'He's dead.' An onlooker called, pointing up at Jesus. Remy could see he was. He lifted his clothing clear from his legs and ran from the hill, leaving his friends and the crowd behind him. He ran as fast as he could from Jesus, from the crucifixions, and from the truth he had stumbled upon on the hill.

They have pierced my hands and feet. They divide my garments among themselves and throw dice for my clothing.
(Psalm 22:16, 18)

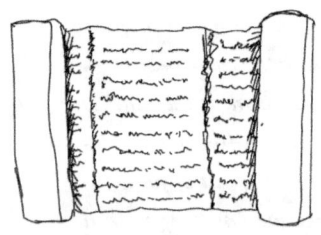

Known

Jesus faced them. He would tell them the truth.

'You say, "He is our God," but you don't even know him.'
Their shocked faces didn't surprise Jesus. He was getting used
to saying things that were unpopular.

'I know him,' he added and his Father's face flashed before
his eyes now. He saw his large hands and remembered the way
he looked at Jesus when they spoke, the feeling of his presence, the sound of his voice, the way his Father held himself
when they sat together. Jesus knew him well.

And these men did not.

'You say, "He is our God," but you don't even know him. I
know him. If I said otherwise, I would be as great a liar as
you! But I do know him and obey him.' (John 8:54–55)

Zippy

Zippy was a field mouse who lived in a cave in the side of a rock. He lived a simple, happy life with not a care in the world besides what to eat for his next meal. The choices were numerous—Zippy could nibble on the plants growing beside his cave or the grass further down the road. There was tree bark galore, and plenty of seeds too. Zippy never went hungry. He slept well in his cave, safe from the weather and from the larger animals who roamed around outside.

Zippy had enjoyed the safety of his cave for many years, and had lived peacefully alone, just the way he liked it … until this morning.

There was somebody new inside his cave, and Zippy didn't know what to make of him. The man had moved in today while Zippy was out nibbling grass, and he was the oddest fellow Zippy had ever seen.

Zippy had seen many people over the years. He always hid from them, but he watched them, and he was accustomed to their ways. This man was different. He was wrapped up in white fabric and so far, he hadn't even moved. He hadn't looked around Zippy's cave, he hadn't spoken a word, he hadn't even gotten down from the bed he'd bought with him. It was very strange and Zippy had never wanted a roommate.

Zippy stayed on the far side of the cave, well away from the strange man, though he kept his eyes on the man at all times. This was definitely the most interesting thing that had ever happened inside his home. The minutes turned into hours and day to night. Meanwhile, Zippy still watched the man. Zippy was frightened to fall asleep. What if the man woke while he was resting? But eventually Zippy nodded off. When he woke the following morning, the man was still lying in the same spot in the same position as the night before.

By the second day, Zippy was growing restless. He wanted his cave back. He wanted the incredibly still—and incredibly boring—fellow to leave. And Zippy had become braver. The man wasn't unpredictable like the other humans Zippy had seen. Instead, he didn't do a thing. So Zippy crept over, very slowly and very cautiously, to get a closer look at him. He sniffed the white cloth wrapped around his arm. The man had a strong odour, but Zippy didn't mind. So did he.

Zippy crawled up onto the fellow's chest and took a look around. It turned out his entire face was covered in the white cloth. How was he managing to breathe in there? Night fell. Morning came. Nothing changed. Night fell again.

Morning came again, the fourth day since Zippy's visitor arrived, and still there was nothing. Zippy wasn't scared of him at all anymore. Instead Zippy was hanging out around the man's head for most of his day.

Zippy had just taken a little nibble of the white cloth covering his face when there was a sudden sound. The stone was being rolled away from the entrance, and light streamed into the cave. Zippy ran for cover and was out of sight in a matter of seconds. He watched from his hiding place. Who could it be? Why, after no visitors for so very long, was Zippy's cave becoming a hot spot of activity? Zippy watched and waited in the shadows.

'Lazarus!' A voice echoed around the cave, bouncing off one wall and hitting the other. Zippy looked to the left and to the right, but saw nothing. Where had the voice come from? Zippy didn't know, but something about the sound of the voice made the hair stand up on the back of Zippy's tail.

'Come out,' the voice said again.

Suddenly, the man covered in the white cloth moved. For the first time in four days, he turned over onto his side and sat up on the bed. Zippy held his breath, watching the man's every move. The man swung his legs off the bed, stood to his feet, and held his hands out before him until he found the wall of Zippy's cave. Lucky for him, Zippy had helped remove some of the cloth from around his eyes. The man followed the wall to the entrance and stepped out into the light.

Zippy was left all alone, sitting in the shadows, watching the man's empty bed, and trying to figure out what on earth that was all about.

Jesus was still angry as he arrived at the tomb, a cave with a stone rolled across its entrance. 'Roll the stone aside,' Jesus told them.

But Martha, the dead man's sister, protested, 'Lord, he has been dead for four days. The smell will be terrible.'

Jesus responded, 'Didn't I tell you that you would see God's glory if you believe?'

Then Jesus shouted, 'Lazarus, come out!' And the dead man came out, his hands and feet bound in graveclothes, his face wrapped in a headcloth. Jesus told them, 'Unwrap him and let him go!' (John 11:38–40, 43–44)

His Corner

The decision had been made. He would be crucified. The soldiers dragged him into the courtyard of the governor's headquarters.

He stood on the concrete floor, barefoot and bloodstained.

The soldier's mocking voices echoed off the high concrete walls.

He was alone now, surrounded by those who were against him.

His back had been torn open, and he couldn't control his trembling.

The soldiers laughed in his face. They found thorns and wove them together, creating a crown. They pushed it into his head.

The blood ran down his face and into his eyes.

They wrapped a purple robe around his shoulders and wrapped his fingers around a stick.

They pretended to worship, bowing down before him.

A soldier grabbed the stick and struck him over the head.

Jesus fell to the ground, his hands hitting the concrete and the weight of the robe falling around him.

The soldiers hooted and laughed, cheering each other on, then yelled at him to stand up.

He struggled to rise. Standing before them, his hands clutched the inside of the robe. The robe was the only corner he had.

Tucked back inside it, he looked out from beneath it, catching glimpses of their faces through the blood in his eyes.

Some of the governor's soldiers took Jesus into their headquarters and called out the entire regiment. They stripped him and put a scarlet robe on him. They wove thorn branches into a crown and put it on his head, and they placed a reed stick in his right hand as a scepter. Then they knelt before him in mockery and taunted, 'Hail! King of the Jews!' And they spit on him and grabbed the stick and struck him on the head with it. (Matthew 27:27–30)

You stand beside me, you hold my hand.

For I hold you by your right hand …
'Don't be afraid. I am here to help you.'
(Isaiah 41:13)

Goldie (continued)

Her bedroom was breathtaking. She sat on her bed to take it all in. Crisp white linen on the bed. Glass walls around her. An inbuilt bath full of steaming water and bubbles, surrounded by candles. Green plants hanging from above. Goldie loved it. She remembered it somehow, like a dream, but knew she'd never seen anywhere so beautiful.

There was a room at the end of the hall. Goldie somehow knew she needed to enter that room last of all. She wandered around the upper level and fell in love with the space he had created for her, the place he had prepared for her.

Now she stepped up to the final door and stood for a minute looking at the door handle. It was a special handle—it held a treasure prepared for this time. She felt a pull and knew it was time. She opened the door and realised it was a child's bedroom. A little girl's bedroom? A girl she would recognise, one she would know well, like the fingerprints on her own hands.

She stepped inside and kneeling down, came face-to-face with a child. A child who looked like her. A child whom she had grieved and missed and remembered. A child she had held in her womb, one she had loved but never met.

Until now. Goldie reached for her and scooped her up into her arms.

The doorbell rang a familiar tune, unlocking a distant memory inside her mind, a memory of a time before Goldie had been conceived. Impossible … but was it?

There was someone outside her front door. She knew who it would be. It was him. He who had prepared a place for her.

'And if I go and prepare a place for you, I will come back and take you to be with me that you also may be where I am.' (John 14:3 NIV)

Arni

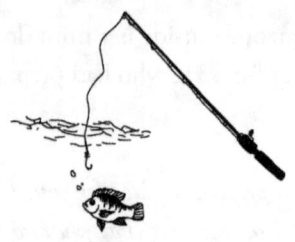

It had been an uncomfortable night for Arni the fish. He had something lodged in his throat and for the life of him, he couldn't remember swallowing anything. It was a peculiar problem, one Arni had never had before. He'd tried everything he could think of to dislodge it, but to no avail. No amount of coughing or swallowing seemed to budge it. Arni could feel that the object was both large and hard. He was sure he would've remembered swallowing something so big, but he could not.

Arni had spent much of the night trying to rectify his unusual problem. In doing so, he had missed out on hours of feeding. Now he was hungry and still very uncomfortable. He swam around in search of food, and soon spotted something that looked tasty dangling in the water above. Arni swooped up to gobble it. No sooner had the snack entered his mouth than Arni found himself attached to it. He could no longer swim freely. Instead, he was being pulled towards the surface, dragged by his mouth. Arni tried with all his might to free himself and to swim away, but he could not. He was well and truly stuck.

Arni was pulled clear out of the water and into the hands of a man standing beside the lake. Arni was shocked and couldn't breathe. The man pulled the hook out from Arni's mouth, and then the oddest thing happened. The man proceeded to dig his fingers right down into Arni's throat!

142

He took hold of the object lodged in Arni's throat and pulled it free. The man stood, looking from the object in one hand, to Arni in the other. 'Unbelievable,' he finally whispered as he shook his head. Then, just like that, he tossed Arni back into the lake.

Arni swam away as fast as he could. What in the world had just happened? Arni had no idea, but he was relieved that his throat was back to normal.

On their arrival in Capernaum, the collectors of the Temple tax came to Peter and asked him, 'Doesn't your teacher pay the temple tax?'

'Yes, he does,' Peter replied. Then he went into the house.

But before he had a chance to speak, Jesus asked him, 'What do you think, Peter? Do kings tax their own people or the people they have conquered?'

'They tax the people they have conquered,' Peter replied.

'Well, then,' Jesus said, 'the citizens are free! However, we don't want to offend them, so go down to the lake and throw in a line. Open the mouth of the first fish you catch, and you will find a large silver coin. Take it and pay the tax for both of us.' (Matthew 17:24–27)

Lost and Found

Why do I doubt you time and time again?
Like those you led out of captivity in Egypt.
Who wandered in the wilderness for forty years.
You set them free, yet they remained lost.
You set me free, yet I remain lost.

> *And I am convinced that nothing can ever separate us from God's love. Neither death nor life, neither angels nor demons, neither our fears for today nor our worries about tomorrow—not even the powers of hell can separate us from God's love.* (Romans 8:38)

Tom

Tom realised before any of the others did, and he felt the blood drain from his face. It had been his only responsibility. Why was he always so forgetful? His mind raced, trying to think up a way to rectify the situation without having to tell the others. But it was hopeless. He'd have to tell them. He waited until Jesus had walked on ahead.

'Guys … I forgot the bread.' He sighed.

'Are you serious?' Drew slowed down beside Tom.

'One minute, I was carrying the bag and the next, we were on the boat and it wasn't with me anymore. I must have left it back on the other side of the lake.' Their expressions said it all. 'I'm sorry.' And he was.

'I have never met anybody who manages to lose things the way you do.' Simon rolled his eyes. The others shook their heads.

'I'm not sure what we'll eat today.' Drew picked up his pace.

'All good, Tom. We'll figure something out.' Phil slapped him on the back.

'And what will that be?' Drew retorted. They all knew it would be hard to come by any food.

'Next time, don't make me hold the bread,' Tom said. He was annoyed with himself and wasn't looking forward to having to tell Jesus when they were all hungry.

Tom glanced up ahead to Jesus. He'd stopped at the side of the road, waiting for them.

'Watch out,' Jesus said as they caught up. 'Beware of the yeast of the Pharisees and Sadducees.'

Great. Jesus already knew Tom had forgotten the bread. And on top of that, he was making sure they didn't accept any bread from the Pharisees or Sadducees. They were in for a long, hungry day. The disciples scowled at Tom and he kicked the dirt with his shoe. He wasn't surprised that Jesus already knew. Perhaps he'd noticed Tom's missing bag. Jesus was very observant.

'Tom, we're going to be starving,' Drew hissed at him. 'You know how much he gives out.' He pointed at Jesus. 'He'll need to refuel.'

'I know, I know, I feel bad enough.' Tom didn't bother trying to defend himself further. He was in for a day of it.

'You have so little faith! Why are you arguing with each other about having no bread?' Jesus turned back to them. He had obviously overheard their conversation. The others looked sheepish and Tom was ashamed.

'Don't you understand yet?' Jesus asked. 'Don't you remember the five thousand I fed with five loaves, and the baskets of leftovers you picked up? Why can't you understand that I'm not talking about bread?'

They were all silent as the realisation settled over them— Jesus wasn't worried about the bread.

'So again I say, beware of the yeast of the Pharisees and Sadducees.'

Later, after they crossed to the other side of the lake, the disciples discovered they had forgotten to bring any bread. At this they began to argue with each other because they hadn't brought any bread. (Matthew 16:5, 7)

700 BC

Isaiah felt the Holy Spirit's presence closely today. He could tell it would be a day of impartation. So he stayed home so as not to be distracted by anything. He would concentrate on God's message. He sat in his home, in his living area on the ground floor, and closed his eyes.

He saw the land of Galilee, the land of the Gentiles, flooded with light. His eyes shot open. That made no sense—the Gentiles weren't God's people. He didn't understand. Yet as Isaiah closed his eyes once more, he saw a great light, brighter than the sun, shining out from the land of Galilee, from where the Gentiles lived beside the sea. The light glowed so brightly that everything it touched no longer sat in darkness. A light so hopeful that everything it touched shone too.

What could the light mean? Who could the light be?

[Jesus] went first to Nazareth, then left there and moved to Capernaum, beside the Sea of Galilee, in the region of Zebulun and Naphtali. This fulfilled what God said through the prophet Isaiah:

'In the land of Zebulun and of Naphtali, beside the sea, beyond the Jordan River, in Galilee where so many Gentiles live, the people who sat in darkness have seen a great light.

And for those who lived in the land where death casts its shadow, a light has shined.' (Matthew 4:13–16)

147

Arva

Arva could hear Snow calling, but she lay still with her eyes closed, savouring the last few moments of rest before she would be found. Snow's footsteps became louder and louder until she exploded into Arva's sleeping room.

'Mama,' Snow exclaimed, out of breath. 'Can you light a lamp? I'm trying to play, and I can't see anymore.' Was it that time already? Arva had rested for longer than anticipated. The baby growing within her womb was taking its toll on her energy levels.

'Yes. I'll be out in just a moment, honey,' she told her daughter as she peeled herself up from her bed. It was time to make dinner. Onie would be home from work soon.

Arva followed the sound of Snow's voice into their living room. Snow was right—it was much too dark to see. Time to light their lamp. Arva groped around in the dark until she found what she was looking for, and lit their lamp.

'Thank you, Mama,' Snow said as she got back to her game on the living room floor. Arva made her way into the kitchen where she reached for one of her baskets. She turned it over a couple of times to be sure it was big enough, then carried it back into the living room. Snow had resumed her game and was happily playing on the floor. Arva crossed the room to the lamp she had lit and placed the basket over the lamp so the room was completely dark once again.

'Mama, I can't see.' Snow said. Arva didn't answer her.

Instead she used the wall to find her way back into the kitchen where she would try to cook dinner in the dark.

'You are the light of the world—like a city on a hilltop that cannot be hidden. No one lights a lamp and then puts it under a basket. Instead, a lamp is placed on a stand, where it gives light to everyone in the house. In the same way, let your good deeds shine out for all to see, so that everyone will praise your heavenly Father.' (Matthew 5:14–16)

Saul

Saul crouched down low, hiding among the baggage. It had been a last-minute decision and not one he was proud of, but he'd panicked. Now he was hidden, he would stay put. He was sure no one would find him here.

His last week had been surreal. At first, he'd been filled with excitement at the prospect of becoming Israel's king. Then the self-doubt had set in.

Saul knew who he really was. He was from the tribe of Benjamin, the smallest tribe in all Israel, and Saul's family was the least important of those tribes. Saul was not a king. Samuel the Seer must have gotten it wrong. Saul was sure his message hadn't come from God.

Saul drew his legs up, resting his chin on his knees, and he waited and listened. The crowd was huge. All the Israelites had gathered to see who God would appoint as king through Samuel the Seer. Well, it wouldn't be Saul. Not any more.

Saul listened as they chose the tribe of Benjamin from among the tribes. His heart beat heavily against his chest. He listened as his own family was called forward from Benjamin's tribe. What would they do if they called for him and discovered he wasn't there? Saul didn't know but he closed his eyes, resting them on his forearms.

Then his name was called. It was Samuel's voice. Saul peeked out from beneath his arms. What would Samuel do now?

If they couldn't find him, would they choose someone else? Saul hoped so.

There was mumbling and confusion amongst the crowd.

'Where is Saul?' someone yelled. The mumbling from the crowd grew louder and louder.

'Quieten down!' Samuel's voice rose above the crowd. 'I will ask the Lord.'

Saul held his legs tightly, and his pulse raced as Samuel spoke to God. Footsteps approached the baggage he was hiding behind. Surely not. Surely Samuel wouldn't find him here?

Moments later, Samuel poked his head over the luggage and looked down at Saul. Saul peered out from beneath his arm. Maybe he could pretend he'd been busy searching for something. No. There was no point. He could see it in Samuel's eyes. Samuel knew he'd been hiding.

'Come on Saul.' Samuel looked at him knowingly and Saul slowly untangled his long, lanky body and stood beside the prophet.

So Samuel brought all the tribes of Israel before the Lord, and the tribe of Benjamin was chosen by lot. Then he brought each family of the tribe of Benjamin before the Lord, and the family of the Matrites was chosen. And finally Saul son of Kish was chosen from among them. But when they looked for him, he had disappeared! So they asked the Lord, 'Where is he?'

And the Lord replied, 'He is hiding among the baggage.' So they found him and brought him out, and he stood head and shoulders above anyone else. (1 Samuel 10:20–23)

Zaza

Zaza was sick and tired of all of the talk about Jesus. She was sick of the crowds, sick of the rumours, and sick of her home town being overrun with sick people trying to find him! She refused to believe there was any good to come of it all. She'd seen this type of thing before. Jesus was just another charismatic leader, the latest fad. No doubt all the sick and hopeful were left disappointed at the end of the day.

She ventured out of her front door, and was greeted by another crowd forming in the street outside of her home. Great! Jesus was obviously in town again. Zaza rolled her eyes. She would ignore them and get through the crowd as fast as she could. She held a piece of bread in one hand, protected under a cloth, to give to Bart as she passed him.

Zaza put her head down and made her way quickly down her street. To her dismay, the crowd seemed to thicken near where Bart sat. Typical! Zaza stopped for a moment to assess the situation and see how best to proceed, but a bystander stepped back and knocked into her. She dropped the bread and cursed beneath her breath.

'I'm sorry.' The man bent down beside her. 'Let me help you'. Zaza held her tongue, fuming. It was best she said nothing. She brushed the dirt from the bread and wrapped it back in its cloth, completely ignoring the stranger. Bart would still appreciate it—he wasn't fussy. Zaza hoped Jesus would leave soon, then all this silly business would end.

She continued on, making her way through the crowd until she reached Bart. He sat on the ground in his usual spot, his coat wrapped around him like a blanket. Bart was blind, and Zaza had grown fond of him over the years he'd begged on the street close to her home.

'I brought you some bread.' She spoke louder than normal, so Bart could hear her over the crowd. Bart held his palm out, but she could tell he was only half listening to her. Great. Even Bart was being swept away with all of this Jesus business. Zaza only hoped he hadn't caught wind of the lies that were circulating.

'How have you been?' Zaza tried again. Usually Bart was eager to chat, but today it seemed like he was on another planet. The crowd around them cheered, as though a buzz of excitement spread through them.

'Jesus is here!' someone yelled. Bart sat up, his coat falling down around his lap, sitting as tall as he could beside Zaza.

'Jesus!' Bart called out.

Zaza jumped back, shocked to hear him shout so loudly.

'Jesus, have mercy on me,' he called. There was a rawness in his voice, a desperation Zaza had never heard from him before.

'Jesus, Son of David, please have mercy on me,' Bart called again. His voice broke this time.

Zaza was furious that this Jesus had fooled so many people. That Bart, her friend, now believed there was some sort of hope to be had, that he would regain his sight. That was utterly impossible.

'Jesus!' Bart yelled so loud this time that Zaza jumped back.

'Be quiet,' she said to Bart. He was screaming in her ear and for what? It was pointless. People were looking at them. Even if there was any chance of Jesus hearing Bart over the crowd, there was absolutely no chance of him restoring Bart's eyesight. Zaza was sure of that.

But Zaza's protesting didn't stop Bart.

'Son of David, have mercy on me!' he called out again. Others in the crowd began to yell back at Bart, telling him to be quiet. It was one thing for her to tell him to hush but she didn't like strangers telling him. She scowled at them and looked back to Bart who continued to yell for Jesus.

She sighed loudly and stood up. If he wanted to talk to this Jesus so badly, then she would help him. She would deal with his disappointment afterwards. But it was clear Bart would not be stopped. Standing on tiptoes, she could see Jesus walking away, the crowd following his every move.

'Jesus!' she called as loudly as she could. Bart reached out his hand, groping for hers, his smile contagious. Zaza smiled despite herself as she took his hand and called out again. Jesus stopped walking and turned around. Zaza lost sight of him over the crowd but called out again, this time in unison with Bart. The crowd moved aside. People turned to face Zaza.

'Cheer up,' a stranger said. 'Come on, he's calling you.'

Bart threw his coat from his lap and jumped up faster than Zaza had ever seen him move. Zaza grasped his hand and led him through the crowd towards Jesus, bracing herself.

What would Bart do when he realised Jesus was just an ordinary man? What would he do when his hopes came crashing down? As they drew closer, Zaza tried to think about what she could say to comfort Bart. She barely looked at Jesus, concentrating on Bart instead. Bart's face shone with expectation and Zaza's heart ached for him.

'What do you want me to do for you?' Jesus asked. Bart swallowed hard, then took a deep breath.

'My rabbi,' he said, his voice quiet and sure. 'I want to see!'

Zaza was right. Bart had been led to believe that this man could heal his sight. This was it. Zaza held her breath and waited. How would Jesus let him down gently?

She couldn't look at Bart, but looked at the dirt around their feet, waiting for Jesus to speak.

'Go, for your faith has healed you,' Jesus said.

What? What did that mean? Zaza didn't know. It was still and silent beside her, then Bart made an odd sound. She slowly looked up from the dirt at their feet and into Bart's eyes ... his eyes that stared straight back into hers. Tears brimmed in his eyes then welled over, streaming down his muddy face as he looked from Zaza to Jesus.

Bart could see.

When Bartimaeus heard that Jesus of Nazareth was nearby he began to shout, 'Jesus, Son of David, have mercy on me!'

'Be quiet!' many of the people yelled at him.

But he only shouted louder, 'Son of David, have mercy on me!'

When Jesus heard him, he stopped and said, 'Tell him to come here.'

So they called the blind man. 'Cheer up,' they said. 'Come on, he's calling you!' Bartimaeus threw aside his coat, jumped up, and came to Jesus.

'What do you want me to do for you?' Jesus asked.

'My Rabbi,' the blind man said, 'I want to see!'

And Jesus said to him, 'Go, for your faith has healed you.' Instantly the man could see, and he followed Jesus down the road. (Mark 10:47–52)

Barry

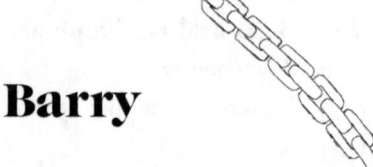

Barry woke with a start, his face leaning on the chains that held him. He must have dozed off momentarily, a miracle considering the state of his captivity.

Barry had dreamt of Hiah again, the young man he'd killed. Hiah had been his friend, but now he was dead. Though Barry had only murdered Hiah once, he had killed him many times in his dreams. He wished the dreams would stop. Barry knew he was a murderer. He didn't need to relive his offences each time he slept.

Barry kept quiet in his prison cell, surrounded by heavy chains, when he realised he could hear voices. They came from outside. He held his breath, straining to hear. Was that Pilate's voice?

'You brought this man to me, accusing him of leading a revolt.' It was! Pilate would be announcing his verdict on Jesus, an important announcement for Barry. One that his life literally hung on. Barry stayed as still and as quiet as he could to listen.

'I have examined him thoroughly on this point in your presence and find him innocent.' Barry's heart dropped. If Jesus was set free, then Barry would be put to death. He knew the tradition—there would only be one prisoner released today.

'Herod came to the same conclusion and sent him back to us,' Pilate continued. 'Nothing this man has done calls for the death penalty. So I will have him flogged, and then I will release him.'

It was a conversation Barry was not supposed to have heard from captivity, but he had heard it. It wasn't good news for Barry. He pulled at his chains, yanking them as hard as he could, desperate for freedom, but it was no use. The chains held him firm. This was it. The day he would die. Hiah's face flashed before his eyes. Perhaps Barry deserved to die … but he didn't want to.

He leaned his head back against the wall and looked up at the ceiling. The crowd was hollering. It sounded like they were going wild out there. What was going on? They would come for him soon to lead him to his death. The crowd began to chant, their voices rising together as one. Barry couldn't make out what it was they were chanting. He sat still trying to listen.

'Kill Jesus and release Barry to us.' Barry sat up straight, his eyes widening. Had he misheard them? Were they calling for his release? But why? They had just been told Jesus was innocent, so why would they choose to release Barry over an innocent man? Barry didn't know, but he didn't care either. It would be the crowd's choice today, and for some unexplainable reason it sounded like today was Barry's lucky day.

'Kill Jesus and release Barry to us.' The words were clear now. Would Barry escape death after all? Would he taste freedom on the outside once more? Anticipation rose as the chanting became louder. A smile slowly made its way across Barry's face.

They wanted him free.

Then a mighty roar rose from the crowd, and with one voice they shouted, 'Kill him and release Barabbas to us!'

(Barabbas was in prison for taking part in an insurrection in Jerusalem against the government, and for murder.) Pilate argued with them, because he wanted to release Jesus. But they kept shouting 'Crucify him! Crucify him!'

For the third time he demanded, 'Why? What crime has he committed? I have found no reason to sentence him to death. So I will have him flogged, and then I will release him.'

But the mob shouted louder and louder, demanding that Jesus be crucified, and their voices prevailed. (Luke 23:18–23)

Tag Team

Jesus embraced him, holding him tight. It was surreal to see him in the flesh. It had been a very long time, a whole lifetime ago in human time, although only a breath in heavenly time. Jesus pulled back and held him by the shoulders. They laughed at each other and Jesus wiped the tears from his cheeks. It had been a long time since Jesus had heard the sound of his laugh.

'It's your turn, my brother,' Jesus said to him. The Holy Spirit nodded in response, a silence stretching out between them. Jesus had completed his work. He had overcome death, and now he would send the Holy Spirit to those who waited for him.

But in fact, it is best for you that I go away, because if I don't, the Advocate won't come. If I do go away, then I will send him to you. (John 16:7)

Family Ties

She was annoyed really. When did he plan on visiting her, his own mother? She was hearing all sorts of stories flying around about him and the great works he was performing, but he had obviously forgotten about his own family. Mary knew she was being oversensitive. She knew that Jesus loved her, naturally.

But she was worried for him, because not everybody who spoke of him spoke favourably. And she was his mother. Of course she worried about him. But if she was honest, she also felt a little left out. He hadn't checked in with his family for some time, and it wasn't like him. His priorities had obviously shifted and by the sounds of things, he had been a very busy boy.

Mary had brought the younger boys along with her. They could visit their brother too. It would be good to see them all together in one place again—it had been a while.

The crowd thickened around the home where Jesus was. Mary would let the boys go ahead to make a way for her. She followed their lead, edging through the crowd little by little as the crowd around them became thicker. There were people everywhere, and they didn't make it far. How frustrating. They had come all this way, and Mary was determined to see her son. She stood on her tiptoes and saw the house entrance was still quite a way off.

'I don't think we'll get in, Mum,' Mary's youngest son said. 'There are too many people.'

Mary was not pleased. All these people were here to see Jesus, but none of these people were his own mother. She had a right to be here and a right to see him! Determination took hold.

'We'll call for him, tell him we are out here,' she said to the boys. They nodded. 'If we can't make it in to see him, then he'll have to come out to meet us.'

Mary backed away from the house and spotted a tree stump. She climbed on top of the stump with the help of her son and finding her balance, let go of his hand.

'Excuse me,' she called out to the gathered crowd. A few people glanced her way, but most continued on as they had been.

'Hello,' she called out. 'Excuse me!' This time, her shout drew more attention.

'My mother has something to say,' her son called out from beside her. He was a good boy. The crowd turned towards Mary.

'Jesus is my son,' she told them. With that, Mary had their full attention. Some people gasped. Others stood in awe before her. Mary knew she was blessed to be his mother. She smiled at the crowd. 'I have come to see Jesus myself, along with his brothers, but we can't get into the house because the crowd is so thick.'

'We will tell him for you,' some people called back from the crowd.

'Thank you,' Mary replied. Perfect! The message took off with the crowd, yelling towards those who stood at the front door. Then the message was taken inside, just like that.

Mary jumped down from the stump and wiped her hands together. Jesus would be out to see them in no time.

Five minutes passed, and Jesus didn't come out. Mary was sure he would be out in just a moment, but an hour went by and there was still no sign of him. He didn't come out of the house to see them. Mary felt a mixture of emotions—surprised, but also annoyed and a bit embarrassed. Eventually Mary gave up. Rounding up her sons, they quietly left the house and the crowds and went home.

Then Jesus' mother and brothers came to see him, but they couldn't get to him because of the crowd. Someone told Jesus, 'Your mother and your brothers are outside, and they want to see you.'

Jesus replied, 'My mother and my brothers are all those who hear God's word and obey it.' (Luke 8:19–21)

He is trustworthy regardless of my circumstances.

'This is my command—be strong and courageous!
Do not be afraid or discouraged.
For the Lord your God is with you wherever you go.'
(Joshua 1:9)

Fox

Herod Antipas was resting when there was a knock at his door. A servant poked his head in.

'Sir, the Pharisees you spoke with this morning have returned.'

Already! That was fast.

'Bring them in,' Herod ordered.

The servant left, closing the door behind him.

Herod had instructed the Pharisees just that morning to find Jesus and to tell him to leave. Get out of here, or Herod would have him killed. But he hadn't expected the men to return so soon. He hoped they brought good news—that Jesus had already left.

The Pharisees followed the servant back into his presence and stood before him.

'Well?' Herod asked.

They looked nervous. Perhaps they hadn't found Jesus after all. If not, why had they returned?

'We found Jesus.' One of the Pharisees finally spoke.

Good. Herod's message had been delivered. No doubt Jesus—fearful for his life—had left the area quick smart.

'What did Jesus say?' Herod asked.

The Pharisee who had spoken hesitated, looking to the man beside him on his left, then at the man on his right. What was going on?

'Tell me. What were his words?'

'We delivered your message,' the Pharisee said, but he faltered, tripping over his words. The man standing to his right took over.

'We delivered your message, and Jesus' exact words were, "Go tell that fox that I will keep on casting out demons and healing people today and tomorrow; and the third day I will accomplish my purpose. Yes, today, tomorrow, and the next day I must proceed on my way. For it wouldn't do for a prophet of God to be killed except in Jerusalem."'

Herod was speechless. Was he mistaken, or had Jesus just called him a fox?

At that time some Pharisees said to him, 'Get away from here if you want to live! Herod Antipas wants to kill you!'
Jesus replied, 'Go tell that fox that I will keep on casting out demons and healing people today and tomorrow; and the third day I will accomplish my purpose.' (Luke 13:31–32)

Vila's Bread

Vila always rose early to get a head start on her bread. While everybody else was still asleep, Vila would measure out her ingredients and add them to her bread trough. She pulled and she pressed, she rolled and she kneaded, then she let her dough sit to rest.

Once the dough had risen, Vila shaped it and formed her loaf. Vila baked her bread to perfection, its aroma rising into the crystal blue sky. She was good at what she did. Though today … when Vila took her golden bread out of the oven and placed it on the cooling ledge, she noticed the loaf leaned a little to the left. It had favoured one side during the baking process. Vila didn't mind. It was beautiful all the same and would still taste delicious.

When the bread had cooled, Vila took her golden loaf and placed it in her store. Town would soon be humming, and Vila would be busy. She was well known in town, her store reliable, her products sought after and enjoyed by many. A bird approached her golden bread, no doubt hoping to snatch a peck, but Vila had her eye on the bird and quickly shooed it away. She had made that mistake before.

The bread sat on the store shelf but not for long. Two men approached Vila, handed over a coin, and purchased the golden loaf. Vila wrapped it in a piece of cloth and just like that, the bread was gone.

The men carried the bread through town, from one stall to another, then into a home. They took the loaf up some stairs, into a light-filled room where the hint of fresh paint lingered. The bread was placed on a large wooden table covered by a linen tablecloth. There, the bread waited for many hours. The two men came and went, adding more items to the table as the day turned to evening. When the sun went down, those who the supper was prepared for arrived. A group of men chatted quietly amongst themselves until the door of the room was closed. Then they relaxed into the room, obviously comfortable in one another's company.

The men sat together around the table, looking at the golden loaf of bread and the wine. Their stomachs rumbled, but they waited.

Jesus reached out a hand, wrapping his fingers around the golden loaf, and lifting it from its resting place. He held the loaf before him with two hands, its aroma rising, the dough soft beneath his fingertips. He looked down at the loaf for a moment—Vila's loaf.

All eyes were on Jesus.

He raised his eyes to the ceiling and thanked God for the bread. Using his thumbs, he pulled the loaf apart, breaking it into pieces, and handing them out to his disciples.

'This is my body, which is given for you,' he told them, speaking of the bread. The bread was his body. 'Do this to remember me.'

They took the bread, now broken into pieces and they ate it, the texture perfect, the flavour exceptional. Each man perplexed, each man accepting his piece of the golden loaf, accepting it as a part of his body. His body that was broken for them.

So the two disciples went into the city and found every-thing just as Jesus had said, and they prepared the Passover meal there.

In the evening Jesus arrived with the twelve disciples.

He took some bread and gave thanks to God for it. Then he broke it in pieces and gave it to the disciples, saying, 'This is my body, which is given for you. Do this in remem-brance of me.' (Mark 14:16–17, Luke 22:19)

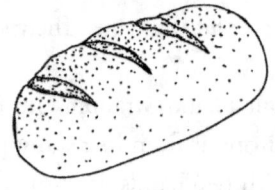

Mystery

He placed something into her hand. It was smooth and round, firm and cool to the touch. She held it in her hand, wrapped in her warm fingers. Before turning away, she peered down to see what it was. Unravelling her fingers from its smooth surface, she saw it was a stone. A white stone—the most beautiful white, both bright and clear. She rolled it over in the palm of her hand a couple of times before she realised there was something engraved in its surface.

It was a name.

Squinting, she read the name written there and gasped. She blinked unbelieving eyes as tears blurred her vision, and she felt as though the breath had been knocked clear from her chest. Clamping her fingers closed around the stone once again, she took deep breaths, one after another. Surely it was the most precious thing she had ever held. But how? How had he known? And then she knew, in that moment, without a doubt.

He knew her.

He really knew her. Unlike anyone had known her before. Every intimate detail, every single piece of her. Like a puzzle falling into place, he revealed pieces she had never understood until now.

And I will give to each one a white stone, and on the stone

*will be engraved a new name that no one understands
except the one who receives it.* (Revelation 2:17)

Alo

The man who hung on the middle cross had done nothing wrong. Alo had heard Pilate say so with his own ears.

Alo hung on the cross next to Jesus. Another criminal, Jez, hung on the far side. The build-up to the crucifixions had left Alo exhausted, but that didn't matter now because he would die up here. He would rest forever.

Alo feared death. He feared God because he hadn't had the chance to make things right—he had never made anything right. Alo had failed at life, and he deserved to be here.

Alo had watched others being killed by crucifixion in the past, but watching hadn't prepared him for this pain. Sweat dripped from his forehead, down his chin, and onto his chest. He yearned for death to come quickly. Unlike Jesus, Alo hadn't been tortured. He was healthy and well, so this could take a while. There was no relief. The only way to breathe was to lift himself up by putting pressure on the nails that held his feet. Alo cursed as he lifted himself once more and tears fell from his eyes.

Alo had never seen such a large crowd attend a crucifixion. He didn't have anyone in the crowd below. His family was ashamed of him. They had given up on him years before.

'So you're the Messiah, are you?' Jez called out from the far cross. Alo turned his head. He could barely see Jez past Jesus' cross, but he could hear him.

Jesus was motionless and didn't answer. Perhaps he had passed out.

'If you're the Messiah, prove it by saving yourself—and us too, while you're at it!' Jez yelled. They had placed a crown of thorns on Jesus' head and a sign above him that said 'King of the Jews'. Their hatred for him was so thick, you could taste it in the air. It hurt to speak, but Alo had to try.

'Don't you fear God even when you've been sentenced to die?' Alo asked Jez, his voice rasping. He felt each and every word. 'We deserve to die for our crimes, but this man hasn't done anything wrong.'

Jez didn't reply and Alo was pleased. He struggled for another breath and yelled out in pain. Alo's crimes were many but surely none deserved this. *Oh God, let me die, let the time pass quickly.*

'You're a king, are you?' a man hollered out from the crowd. 'If so, then save yourself. If you're the chosen one from God, come down from your cross.'

The crowd laughed and taunted. It was clear that they were largely present for this reason.

Alo turned his head once more and watched Jesus beside him. His eyes were open now, his body bathed in blood.

'Jesus,' Alo called. Jesus turned his face, and his eyes met Alo's. Breath caught in Alo's throat. He had called out to Jesus and he wasn't sure why. He struggled to take another breath.

'Remember me when you come into your kingdom.' It was an odd thing to say, but Alo would hedge his bets, just in case. He had nothing to lose. Absolutely nothing. He didn't deserve to be remembered, even if Jesus was the Messiah and really did have a kingdom to claim.

'I assure you, today you will be with me in paradise,' Jesus said.

Jesus had no reply for Jez and no reply for the crowd who hollered at him, but he had replied to Alo. *Paradise.* Alo played the word over and over as the minutes became hours, until the very end.

One of the criminals hanging beside him scoffed, 'So you're the Messiah, are you? Prove it by saving yourself—and us, too, while you're at it!'

But the other criminal protested, 'Don't you fear God even when you have been sentenced to die? We deserve to die for our crimes, but this man hasn't done anything wrong.' Then he said, 'Jesus, remember me when you come into your Kingdom.'

And Jesus replied, 'I assure you, today you will be with me in paradise.' (Luke 23:39–43)

Oza

Oza was a swallow who had passed from life through death and would now dwell in a new place.

Oza's creator was nearby. She hadn't seen him, but she could feel him.

From the moment Oza arrived, she knew she belonged. Nowhere had ever felt so warm, so welcoming, so right.

Now she was here, she needed to find somewhere to build her home.

Oza decided to take a look around from above. She flew up high and scanned her surroundings, in search of a home.

She flew far to the left and then back to the right and everything she saw was good, but she saw nowhere to settle, nowhere to make her own.

Oza began to worry. What if she was unable to find a place to call her own?

As Oza flew back and forth, she was aware that she was consistently drawn back to his altar. His golden altar, the place where he dwelt.

She decided to take a closer look.

Oza landed a safe distance away, without making a sound. She eyeballed the golden altar. It was magnificent.

Drawn forward, Oza cautiously approached his altar.

Could she come near? Would she be welcome?

Oza edged ever so quietly closer and closer. Suddenly, she saw it and froze.

Nestled in beside his altar, tucked into an alcove, the bones of a nest had been laid. Oza's heart skipped a beat at the sight of the nest.

Who did it belong to? Oza didn't know, but she couldn't take her eyes from the nest. It was positioned perfectly. It was safe and inviting. Most importantly, it was close to him.

As Oza watched the nest, his presence settled around her, and he whispered her name.

Oza stood, staring at the nest and listening to her name on his lips. All at once, she realised … the nest was meant for her.

Oza was home and her heart leapt for joy. She knew it was almost time—she would lay her eggs soon. So she got to work, completing the building of her nest beside his altar. His altar, where she belonged.

How lovely is your dwelling place, O Lord of heaven's armies.

I long, yes, I faint with longing to enter the courts of the Lord.

With my whole being, body and soul, I will shout joyfully to the living God.

Even the sparrow finds a home, and the swallow builds her nest and raises her young at a place near your altar,

O Lord of Heaven's Armies, my King and my God!

What joy for those who can live in your house, always singing your praises. (Psalm 84:1–4)

Cleo

The treetops rustled high up above them as they walked beneath their leafy shade, the path worn and trampled, their spirits heavy and crushed with grief.

'Who could have taken his body?' Cleo asked again. It wasn't really a question any more, although he had asked it many times since they'd left Jerusalem. Zion didn't answer, and Cleo knew why. Zion didn't know anymore than he did. They were both clueless and confused.

'I can't figure it out,' Zion finally said, shaking his head. 'It doesn't make any sense.'

Cleo sighed. The grief had been one thing, but now they had a missing body and it was overwhelming.

'Do you want some water?' Cleo offered the bottle to Zion and the men stopped for a moment to drink. Cleo heard footsteps. Odd. There had been no one for miles. He watched the path cautiously, and a stranger soon rounded the bend.

'Hello, there.' The stranger greeted Cleo and Zion.

'Hello,' Cleo said.

Zion swallowed his mouthful of water and waved to the man.

The stranger joined them as they continued on their way. Cleo raised his eyebrows slightly at Zion, surprised.

'Would you like some water?' Cleo asked the stranger.

'No, thank you.' The stranger replied. He seemed familiar,

though Cleo didn't know him. Cleo sensed no reason to fear the man.

'What were you discussing so intently as you walked along?' the stranger asked.

How had the stranger known they'd been talking? Had he been following them, and they hadn't noticed? They had been deep in conversation, but surely not so much so that they didn't hear a fellow traveller?

'We were discussing what has gone on the last couple of days in Jerusalem,' Cleo replied. It was all anyone was talking about. The stranger was blank, his face unresponsive. Surely he had heard about it …

'What things?' the stranger asked.

'You must be the only person in Jerusalem who hasn't heard.' Cleo's heart ached just thinking about it.

'About Jesus?' Cleo asked.

The man shook his head.

It was clear the man had no idea what he was talking about. Incredible! Did he live under a rock?

Cleo and Zion took turns telling the stranger about Jesus, about how they'd hoped he was the Messiah, how he had died, how his body had disappeared that very morning. Cleo, passionate as he spoke about Jesus, choked up and his eyes filled with tears. He blinked them away, looking down to the ground at his dusty feet until his sandals became clear again. There was something therapeutic about relaying the events, about telling somebody who wasn't there.

The stranger listened but didn't say much. It was a lot to digest all in one go. Their retelling of the tragedy drew to an end, and the three men walked in silence.

'You foolish people!' the stranger said quietly.

'Excuse me?' Cleo asked. Did he just call them foolish? Cleo must have misheard him.

'You find it so hard to believe all that the prophets wrote in the scriptures.' He ignored Cleo. 'Wasn't it clearly predicted that the Messiah would have to suffer all these things before entering his glory?'

Cleo was speechless, as was Zion. Who was this man? Did he know more than he had let on? Did he know something they did not? The stranger talked on, picking out scriptures about Jesus that had been written long before Jesus was born.

'David spoke of the Messiah in the book of psalms, about how his hands and feet would be pierced with nails, about the soldiers who would gamble for his clothing and about how the Messiah would not be left among the dead, but would rise again.'

The stranger went on and on. As he spoke, Cleo's heart felt as though it was burning, as though there were a fire raging within his chest. Cleo glanced at Zion, his friend's expression mirroring his own. They both listened, speechless.

As the stranger spoke, time seemed to fly by. Before Cleo knew it, they were nearing the gates of Emmaus, their destination. Cleo couldn't take his eyes off the stranger, unable to believe the man's incredible knowledge of the ancient scriptures. Cleo had only ever known one other who held such wisdom, one other whose words had Cleo's heart burning inside his chest—Jesus.

When the stranger realised the men were stopping at Emmaus, he bid them farewell. A panic rose up inside of Cleo.

'Please, come with us. It is late. You can continue your journey in the morning.' Cleo tried not to sound desperate, but he couldn't help it. He needed the stranger to stay with them, although he didn't know why.

The stranger didn't take much convincing to follow them into the house. When they sat down to eat, he took the bread, blessed it, and broke it.

Zion inhaled sharply beside him as they watched the stranger's hands break the bread. He handed a piece to Cleo and another to Zion. Something like scales fell from Cleo's eyes and he saw the stranger clearly for the first time.

It was him. It was Jesus.

They said to each other, 'Didn't our hearts burn within us as he talked with us on the road and explained the Scriptures to us?' (Luke 24:32)

Merri

It sat there on her dresser, a constant reminder of the love they had shared, and of her heartbreak. It had been payment for her to go away, to leave him alone, so he could live his life with his wife and children.

Merri couldn't move on. She had never known love until she'd known Azel. Merri had known of the act of love—her profession—but never love itself. They hadn't seen it coming. Azel had hired Merri for one thing alone. But as time went on and his visits became regular, she found herself waiting for him.

Merri had fallen in love with Azel, and when his wife discovered them, Merri knew he'd thought about leaving her to be with Merri. But he had children, wealth, and a reputation to uphold. And Merri wasn't enough. Azel left her with a broken heart, and an expensive gift—an alabaster jar filled with fine perfume.

But Merri couldn't escape him. Everywhere she turned, his memory haunted her. Some days, she felt as though sanity was slipping away, seeping out through her fingertips. The townspeople called her crazy and Merri couldn't defend herself. She was losing her mind.

When Azel left and told her he would never speak to her again, she'd been found roaming the streets at night. She'd dreamed she'd been searching for Azel in the dead of the night, but her dreams had somehow crossed with reality. It happened over and over again.

Then there was the guilt. It haunted her—Azel's wife, and the look in her eyes when she'd discovered them. That look now mirrored Merri's own heartbreak. Merri was sorry for the pain she had caused. She yearned for him. Yet in the same breath, she was filled with guilt over what they had done.

Now Merri sat on her unmade bed, hugging her knees to her chest. Her makeup would be running. She should fix it, but she didn't care. Instead she stared at the jar on her dresser, yearning for the love she had lost.

Another face flashed before her eyes. Jesus.

That had been happening a lot lately, and she didn't know why. She had only ever seen him from a distance, but he called to her—not with his voice, but inside her mind. It sounded crazy and perhaps it was. But whenever she passed him on the road or saw him in town, she heard him. He told her to come to him. She never listened. Instead, she ran the other way. She would stay away from Jesus. She would never go to him. She would cling to her memories of Azel forever, until she died. She wouldn't risk anyone taking her memories.

Merri peeled herself off the bed and fetched some water to clean her face. She would need to reapply her makeup before work, but she'd head into town first. It was Tuesday, and Azel visited town on Tuesday. The chance to set eyes on him, even just for a moment, was reason enough to venture out.

The day was clear, and Merri walked the short distance to town in the sun. She would keep to herself. The townspeople had judged her long ago, not just because of her wandering throughout the night or the question around her sanity but because she had been publicly put to shame after her relationship with Azel. Although the weather was warm, Merri pulled her shawl over her face and entered the marketplace, wanting to go unnoticed.

The marketplace was busy. Merri kept her head down and, peering through the gap in her shawl, concentrated on finding Azel. It was the only reason she had come. Minutes went by and she wandered past one stall and stopped in front of another, when she saw them.

'Daddy, can we get apples?' A child bolted in front of Merri, and she lost her balance. As she struggled to remain upright, she realised whose child had tripped her. Azel moved fast. He let go of his wife's arm and darted to the ground where he caught Merri in his arms just before she hit the ground. Merri inhaled sharply, his face close to hers.

'I'm so sorry,' Azel said. 'Are you ok?'

Azel's wife scolded the child.

Merri remained speechless. He didn't know who she was.

Her eyes filled with tears and locked with his. She choked on a reply, as recognition, then terror swept over his face. Merri's shawl fell back from her neck and Azel froze. Merri looked to his wife, who pulled their child into a hug, covering his eyes with her hands. Azel looked from his wife to Merri.

Then he did the unthinkable. He dropped her. Merri fell to the ground with a thud as Azel stood, shaking her off his hands. He put his arm back around his wife and they hurried away.

Merri's heart pounded so hard against her chest that she thought it might explode. Deep shame fell over her as she picked herself up, lifted her skirts, and ran. Tears flew from her cheeks as she ran out of town, down a lonely road with no one in sight. She ran until her lungs felt like they would explode, then stopped and leaned against a tree trunk. She sobbed, a gut-wrenching noise, a sound she had never heard before. And she decided. She would die soon. It was a relief to finally make the call.

When Merri arrived home, she sank into bed, exhausted, but sure that tomorrow she would end her life. She fell into a deep sleep and dreamed she was wandering the quiet streets, walking down dark roads, but she kept falling. Each time her hands hit the ground, she saw his eyes.

She cried out in her sleep, rising to her feet once more. She needed to stop falling, to stay upright, but she couldn't. She fell again. This time, her head broke her fall, waking her.

It had happened again. She was no longer in her bed. Instead, she lay on the road in town in the middle of the night. She blinked once, twice. Although awake, she still saw eyes before her. Was he here? Was it Azel?

Merri pushed herself up, her head pounding from where it had hit the ground, and she looked up into the face of the man standing above her. Jesus. He held out his hand to her.

'I'm tired.' She struggled to speak through her sobs. 'I'm so tired.'

'I can help you,' he said simply. Merri reached out and put her hand into his. It surprised her—she hadn't wanted to, but he was here, and she had run out of options. She was about to end her life, and was walking through the streets in the middle of the night. Did he know she would be here? How could he ever help her?

She stood before him now, her hands inside his. He said nothing, but something was happening. A warmth slowly but surely trickled over her, like a gentle peace. It began in her fingertips and moved up her hands and arms. Before long, her entire body burned with its warmth. Azel's face flashed before her eyes and she blinked painfully, cutting eye contact with Jesus, but he took his hand and held it to her forehead. The memory of her love for Azel, of her guilt and shame, lost its sting. Nothing happened but everything changed. Merri's eyes opened wide as she looked back into his. She felt joy, a joy so intense, so surreal that it surpassed anything she had ever felt.

'Go home,' he told her. Merri silently wept as she walked. What had he done to her? How had he shifted things inside her heart and mind with only a touch?

Merri stepped into her bedroom, the room she didn't remember leaving. Freedom was all she felt. It overwhelmed her. She looked at her alabaster perfume jar and with the memories there was nothing—only peace.

All through the day, all she thought of was Jesus. He had saved her. She owed him her life. Evening approached, and she felt drawn to find him. She eyeballed her perfume jar— she wanted to take it with her. How silly. It was the most valuable thing that she owned.

But the pull was so strong, she struggled to leave home without it. So she took it from her dresser and went to find him. She only had to ask a couple of people to learn where he was. Once she arrived at the house, she stopped and took a deep breath before entering the front door. When she stepped inside, he looked up from the dining table as though he'd been waiting for her.

She kept her eyes on Jesus as she rounded the table, ignoring those seated beside him. As she looked into his eyes he smiled, just slightly, a knowing smile that encouraged her. He looked to her perfume jar and she knew what to do. She took her jar and broke it against the side of the table. She wouldn't just open it. She would give it all to Jesus, not saving any for herself. Without Jesus, Merri's life would have been over by now. She owed him everything.

She took the broken jar and poured perfume over his head until the jar was almost empty. It dripped from his hair, down his arms. Then she kneeled before him and poured the last of the perfume over his feet. Her tears dripped from her chin, mingling with the perfume on his feet.

'Why waste such expensive perfume?' Merri heard a man say. 'It could have been sold for a year's wages and the money given to the poor.'

'Leave her alone,' Jesus told him. 'Those who are forgiven a little, love a little. And those who are forgiven much?' He looked into Merri's eyes. 'They love a lot.'

She was forgiven. Her sins were many, but Jesus had set her free. Free from her guilt, and free from her love for Azel.

'She has prepared my body for burial,' Jesus said. 'Wherever the good news is preached throughout the world, this woman's deed will be remembered too.'

When a certain immoral woman from that city heard he was eating there, she brought a beautiful alabaster jar filled with expensive perfume. Then she knelt behind him at his feet, weeping. Her tears fell on his feet.

'I tell you, her sins—and they are many—have been forgiven, so she has shown me much love. But a person who is forgiven little shows only little love.' (Luke 7:37–38, 47)

He who created my pain threshold tells me not to fear.

Even when I walk through the darkest valley,
I will not be afraid, for you are close beside me.
(Psalm 23:4)

Eben

Eben was honoured to have been chosen as one of the seventy-two. He had watched the twelve over recent months and had ached to be one of them. It seemed everywhere Jesus went and everything he touched became better. Eben wanted to be included in whatever it was that Jesus was doing.

It was very dark tonight. The moon was but a slither, and Eben and Roi were almost home. It had been a month since Jesus had sent them out into the unknown with detailed instructions and a clear message. Eben felt butterflies in his stomach when he thought of relaying their many adventures of the past month to Jesus. He was so ready to tell Jesus about all they had seen and done.

'Not long now.' Roi grinned, his white teeth standing out against the darkness. 'Shall we run the rest of the way?'

'Let's go,' Eben replied. The pair picked up their pace until they finally arrived at the house where Jesus was staying. There was a candle burning inside—maybe Jesus would still be awake.

Panting and out of breath, Eben pushed open the door and was welcomed by Jesus. He rose from his seat and moved to the entrance, embracing Eben and then Roi. Others had already arrived and were seated around the room. The house was buzzing, their excitement to relay all that had happened bubbling over. When Eben and Roi were seated and had greeted the others, Jesus quietened the room, and nodded

187

at Eben. Eben grinned. He didn't know where to begin. He had never felt so full, never felt such a sense of pride and belonging.

'It was something else.' Eben was encouraged to see those around him nodding in agreement. Eben looked Jesus in the eyes.

'Lord,' Eben said, surprised when his voice cracked. 'Even the demons obeyed us when we used your name.' Eben shook his head in disbelief and a tear escaped, rolling down his cheek. He used the back of his hand to wipe it away.

Jesus nodded, a twinkle in his eye. In his entire life, Eben had never felt joy the way he did right now, in this moment. They had been called to do a good work. They had completed the task set out before them, and they had made Jesus proud of them.

***

Rage consumed him, power had been taken from him. God's son had given mere humans authority over his dark power. He screamed a mighty roar and violently spun, knocking things over as he moved across the room. Those around him vanished into the background. All knew better than to stay near when he lost composure. He was unpredictable at the best of times, a liar, evil through and through. He would not take it lightly that he had been deprived of what belonged to him. Fury consumed every part of his being. He needed to let off steam. He threw himself down towards the earth forming lightning across the sky.

***

His fingers–firm and strong, steady and sure–took to the register, as he added their names, one after another. He spoke their names out loud as he drew each letter–adding their names to his list of life.

The Lord now chose seventy-two other disciples and sent them ahead in pairs to all the towns and places he planned to visit.

When the seventy-two disciples returned, they joyfully reported to him, 'Lord, even the demons obey us when we use your name!'

'Yes,' he told them, 'I saw Satan fall from heaven like lightning! Look, I have given you authority over all the power of the enemy, and you can walk among snakes and scorpions and crush them. Nothing will injure you. But don't rejoice because evil spirits obey you; rejoice because your names are registered in heaven.' (Luke 10:1, 17–20)

Olive

He was coming! Olive and her mother stood to the side of the road and watched as the people laid their garments on the road. He would soon ride right over them.

He was still far off, but Olive could see him if she stood on her tiptoes. He rode a donkey. Olive's mother squeezed her hand, and Olive's heart beat hard inside her chest.

So many people had gathered. They talked and hollered, sang and clapped. Olive felt shy around people because she was used to staying at home. She was pleased to be visiting the city, but she was filled with a mixture of nerves and excitement. Her eyes were wide as she watched them all. She stood beside her mother and remained quiet.

There was dust swirling high in the hot sun with all the commotion. Olive coughed and waved her free hand in front of her face.

Some people were breaking off tree branches and laying them over the road too. It was fascinating.

Olive was wearing her favourite cloak. She'd chosen it especially because she wanted to look her best for the trip to town. But now a part of her wished she hadn't. As she watched the crowds of people laying their clothing on the road before Jesus, she realised she wanted to lay her cloak down as well.

Olive was sure Mother wouldn't mind. Olive had never seen her mother so consumed by anyone as she was by Jesus.

They had watched him perform miracles that were out of this world. But it wasn't just the thought of giving up her favourite cloak that held her back. The thought of stepping out in front of all these people to lay her cloak on the road … that was terrifying.

Olive looked up at her mother and saw teardrops making a path down her dusty face. Something stirred in Olive's belly. Jesus was getting closer. Olive could see his legs rubbing roughly against the donkey's side. She could see his face through the dust and his smiling eyes. He looked as if he had a purpose as he watched the city ahead. As if he had a plan. She wondered what the plan was.

Suddenly, she didn't care about her favourite cloak anymore. She didn't even care about the crowds pressing in all around her. She wanted to lay her cloak on the road for Jesus. So she would. She would be brave. But she needed to move fast.

She pulled her hand free from her mother's and slipped off her cloak. Her mother looked at her, surprised. She must have realised what Olive was doing, because she kissed Olive's forehead, encouraging her on.

Olive zipped through the crowd to lay her cloak on the road. She spread it out beside a large tree branch just before Jesus arrived. Jesus' donkey veered to the right, and Jesus rode right over the top of Olive's cloak. She stood up to watch him pass.

'Who is this?' the boy standing beside Olive asked as Jesus rode past them.

'It's Jesus, the prophet from Nazareth in Galilee,' Olive replied. She didn't usually speak to strangers, but today she was brave.

Olive grinned back at her mother, elated. She had done it.

Most of the crowd spread their garments on the road ahead of him, and others cut branches from the trees and spread them on the road. Jesus was in the centre of the procession, and the people all around him were shouting,

'Praise God for the Son of David! Blessings on the one who comes in the name of the Lord! Praise God in highest heaven!'

The entire city of Jerusalem was in an uproar as he entered. 'Who is this?' they asked.

And the crowds replied, 'It's Jesus, the prophet from Nazareth in Galilee.' (Matthew 21:8–11)

John

It had finally happened. John felt like he'd been waiting forever. He'd been baptising people in the river day after day after day, waiting all the while. The message God had given him played through his mind day in and day out.

'The one on whom you see the Spirit descend and rest is the one who will baptise with the Holy Spirit.'

John had no idea what that even meant, but he had kept his eye out for it all the same, eager and excited to see.

Then yesterday, it had happened. When John baptised a man named Jesus, he'd pulled him up out of the water and the Spirit had fallen on him. The Spirit was beautiful. John knew the Spirit well, though never with his human eyes. Just the memory made him stop in his tracks. His eyes had seen the Spirit of the Lord, his life's work was complete, and he was overwhelmed with emotion.

He stood now on the side of the riverbank. He would continue to baptise people until he was told otherwise. He still could not believe it had happened–he had baptised the Messiah. A crowd was forming beside the river, and he watched the people as they huddled together, whispering and watching.

Suddenly John saw Jesus walking towards him, and he turned to face him. John had been preparing for Jesus for his entire life. It was surreal. Time stood still as he looked into his face.

'Look,' John told the gathered people as he pointed towards Jesus. 'The Lamb of God who takes away the sin of the world!' The crowd turned, following John's pointed finger. 'He is the one I was talking about when I said, "A man is coming after me who is far greater than I am, for he existed long before me." I did not recognise him as the Messiah, but I have been baptising with water so that he might be revealed to Israel.' The people turned their attention from John to Jesus and watched as he walked towards them.

Then John testified, 'I saw the Holy Spirit descending like a dove from heaven and resting upon him. I didn't know he was the one, but when God sent me to baptise with water, he told me, "The one on whom you see the Spirit descend and rest is the one who will baptise with the Holy Spirit." I saw this happen to Jesus, so I testify that he is the Chosen One of God.' (John 1:32–34)

Golgotha

He was here. His head pounded, and pain roared through his body. He stood on the hill. There were people everywhere. He had thought about this moment, imagined it so many times, and now here he was. He stood, dried blood covering his body. He had made it. He breathed, feeling the air go down deep into his lungs. It would be gone soon. His hands hung limp at his sides as he watched them throw the cross to the ground at his feet. His heartbeat thumped louder and louder in his ears in anticipation of the nails and of the lifting up. He was shoved from behind and fell to his knees. He would not stand again until he had defeated death. They stretched out his hands and his feet and laid him on his cross.

When they came to a place called The Skull, they nailed him to the cross. (Luke 23:33)

Hally

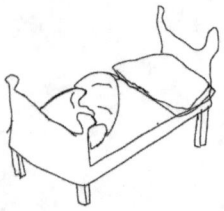

Hally had saved everything she'd earned. She'd sat in the room, waiting for the doctor, feeling her whole life hang on this procedure. If she could be healed, then she could be married. Joah had loved her but couldn't marry a sick woman.

Hally remembered the appointment as if it were yesterday—the doctor's footsteps, her throbbing chest, her hands full of coin pouches, and her heart full of innocent hope.

But the procedure hadn't worked. Nor had anything else. Hally had run out of money and run out of hope. She was well acquainted with the sight of blood. It was so long since the bleeding had started.

Hally had lost her chance at love. The life she had dreamed of with Joah was a distant memory.

Her illness forced her to live in a constant state of fatigue. Jewish law taught that bleeding made her unclean, so Hally was not welcome in the temple. Her only companion in life was Hazzel, her sister.

Hally lay on her bed now. She often napped during the day, but she felt restless this afternoon.

Hally stared at her hands curled beside her face. The skin wasn't as tight as it had once been. A tear made its way down her cheek. Her life had passed her by, slipping through her fingers.

'Hally!' Hazzel burst through the door. She stopped short.

'Sorry. Were you sleeping?'

'No, I can't sleep,' Hally said. Hazzel looked excited.

'You need to get up,' Hazzel said.

'Why?' she asked, surprised.

'Because he's here!' Hazzel clapped her hands.

'Who's here?' Hally didn't want company.

'Jesus is here!' Hazzel's eyes danced. 'The healer I was telling you about. He's in town.'

Hally laid her head back down. She had heard about Jesus, but her hopes had been crushed too many times. She knew better than to trust in him or anyone else.

Hally listened as Hazzel shared the rumours she'd heard. How Jesus had healed a demon-possessed man on the other side of the lake.

Hally didn't want to get her hopes up, not under any circumstances. But as Hazzel spoke, hope rose within Hally, despite herself. She fought against it.

'He wouldn't be able to help me,' she said in a matter-of-fact tone. 'It's been twelve years. Some things can't be helped.'

'We need to move fast, Hal. We don't want to miss him.' Hazzel's eyes were full of hope. Hally didn't want to argue, so she got up and prepared herself to walk to town, which was easier said than done.

Hazzel ran ahead, pulling Hally along. It wasn't hard to find Jesus—he was on the shore, surrounded by a crowd. Hally was nervous. She shouldn't be here.

As they joined the crowd, a man raced past. Hazzel and Hally stood back and watched as he dropped to his knees before Jesus.

'My daughter is dying,' he told Jesus. 'Please come and lay your hands on her; so she can live.'

Hally couldn't believe what she was hearing. How could this man have such belief in Jesus? If his daughter was dying, surely there was nothing that could be done.

But the way he spoke, Hally could tell he did have hope in Jesus. And hope rose in Hally's chest, pushing its way up until tears pricked her eyes.

Jesus nodded at the weeping father.

'I will come.' He rose to follow the man. Hally looked at Hazzel, who kissed her cheek.

'Go, Hally. Follow him.' With that, she was off, off on a mission to speak with Jesus.

Hally wove her way through the people, moving faster than she had in years.

She edged her way closer to Jesus. She passed everyone in the crowd, one by one, until there was only a single family separating her from Jesus.

Hally huffed and puffed, out of breath. She kept her eyes low and could see his sandals up ahead.

She was acutely aware of the power of his presence, but was too afraid to call out to him. How would she get his attention?

A quiet thought out of nowhere whispered in her ear.

Maybe it would be enough if she could reach out and touch Jesus. If he was as powerful as the rumours said, then Hally should try.

She watched his robe, the hem swaying back and forth. It was so close. If she just reached out, she could touch it. So she did.

Hally lightly touched the fabric. Something changed within her body. She couldn't be sure, but the bleeding seemed to stop. The pain disappeared—that she was sure about. Hally gasped.

Jesus spun around, and Hally ducked behind a large man. Had she really been healed?

The pain was gone. A feeling she hadn't experienced in a long time. But why had Jesus stopped? Could he know what Hally had done?

'Who touched my robe?' he asked. Hally cowered in her hiding place. People whispered in the crowd.

'Look at this crowd pressing around you. How can you ask, "Who touched me?"' a man asked Jesus. Hally trembled. It was clear he knew. Who was this man? And could simply touching him have healed her?

Hally's heart hammered and her mouth was dry as she stepped out. She stood before Jesus. She stared at his sandals, then fell to the ground at his feet.

'It was me. I touched you.' Tears welled over and fell from her face. Jesus knelt down and lifted Hally's face.

'Daughter, your faith has made you well.' The look in his eyes took Hally's breath away.

'Go in peace. Your suffering is over.'

A woman in the crowd had suffered for twelve years with constant bleeding. She had suffered a great deal from many doctors, and over the years she had spent everything she had to pay them, but she had gotten no better. In fact, she had gotten worse. She had heard about Jesus, so she came up behind him through the crowd and touched his robe. For she thought to herself, 'If I can just touch his robe, I will be healed.' Immediately the bleeding stopped, and she could feel in her body that she had been healed of her terrible condition. (Mark 5:25–29)

Toah

When David had asked Toah to mind his sheep for him, the day before yesterday, David had said he'd only be gone for a few days. Toah had agreed without hesitation. After all, David had watched the flock for Toah just last week when he'd been unwell and needed to rest at home. They'd been friends since they were children and could rely on each other for help with their sheep.

Now, Toah was stunned as he sat down in the grass beside the sheep—all of them, both his father's sheep and David's. Toah couldn't believe the report he'd just heard about what had taken place between David and a giant of the Philistine army. Would David ever come home again?

David's father, Jesse, had asked David to go to the valley of Elah to deliver food to his brothers who were with Saul and the Israelite army fighting against the Philistines. David had been excited about the trip—there'd been a sparkle in his eyes as they'd talked, and Toah was happy to help his friend.

Toah loved David. There had always been something special about David. He was both quiet and thoughtful but brave and capable at the same time. Toah had heard David's stories—one about when he fought a lion to protect his sheep, and another about fighting a bear. Though his stories were hard to believe, Toah believed them. David wouldn't lie.

David spoke of the God he served often, the God of Israel. David loved God and the way he talked about him over the years had intrigued Toah. He would ask David question after question about the God of Israel, and David never grew tired of answering them.

Toah picked at the grass around his legs. But a giant? A Philistine giant? It was unbelievable. Yet Toah had heard just that morning that David had defeated a giant from the Philistine army using only a sling and a stone. Toah was in shock. He needed to speak with Jesse, to be sure the rumours were true. But at the same time, he knew in his heart that if anyone could defeat a giant, it was David and his God, the God of Israel.

So David left the sheep with another shepherd and set out early the next morning with the gifts, as Jesse had directed him.

But David persisted. 'I have been taking care of my father's sheep and goats,' he said. 'When a lion or bear comes to steal a lamb from the flock, I go after it with a club and rescue the lamb from its mouth. ... I have done this to both lions and bears, and I'll do it to this pagan Philistine, too, for he has defied the armies of the living God! The Lord who rescued me from the claws of the lion and the bear will rescue me from this Philistine!'
(1 Samuel 17:20, 34–37)

Love

Love and Laney were angels of the most High God. After forty days of watching Jesus starving in the wilderness, they had finally been released to help him this morning. Love had been ready for days, and everything they would need was prepared and ready to go. Jesus had more than proved himself. He was willing to give it all, holding nothing back. They had watched as the devil had tried to tempt him with food, power, and prestige. But Jesus had turned the devil down. Love knew his father would be proud.

Love grasped Laney's hand inside her own and held the equipment in the other. Laney smiled at Love and they left, journeying from their home above, down to earth and into the wilderness to Jesus. He lay on a rock, his body frail and weak, fading away, his bones protruding from beneath his skin.

Love rushed to his side and held her hands to his face. Jesus opened his eyes but didn't move. Love could tell he was dehydrated. They needed to lower his temperature. Love nodded at Laney, who opened their bag and pulled out a drip. Laney attached the IV line into the back of his hand. Love placed a compress over his forehead and a piece of ice beneath his tongue. Then they waited.

The bag emptied its contents into his veins, and Love breathed a sigh of relief as they watched the fluids doing their magic and the colour returning to his cheeks. Love had missed him. They both had. Laney knelt beside him, leaned down and kissed his cheek.

Then the devil went away, and angels came and took care of Jesus. (Matthew 4:11)

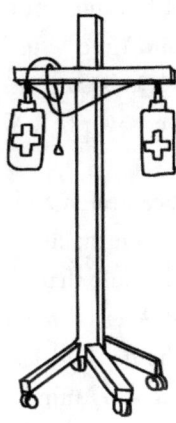

Beach Fire

Peter sat with Jesus on the beach. He could feel the sand beneath his feet and salt against his cheeks. The fire burned low between them, and the smell of cooked fish lingered in the air. This was the third time Jesus had appeared to them since he'd been killed. It was surreal. They sat quietly with him, hanging on his every word … although he hadn't said much so far.

When the fish had been eaten and they'd all had their fill of bread, Jesus sat back from the fire and turned to Peter.

'Peter, do you love me more than these?' Jesus asked.

The breath caught in Peter's throat as he looked into Jesus' eyes. The memory of the fire he'd sat beside the night Jesus was arrested shot through his mind, along with the words he'd heard and spoken.

You're not one of that man's disciples, are you? he'd been asked.

No, I am not, he'd replied. Now regret sat heavy in the pit of his stomach.

'Yes, Lord,' he replied as his eyes filled with tears. 'You know I love you.'

Peter searched Jesus' face. What had he meant, asking Peter that? Surely Jesus knew Peter loved him, but did Jesus know how sorry he was? Of the guilt he'd carried since that night? Peter swallowed the lump forming in his throat.

'Then feed my lambs,' Jesus said quietly.

'Peter, do you love me?' Jesus asked for the second time.

Instantly, Peter was back there again. He saw the woman's face, the woman who had let him inside the gate.

You're not one of his disciples, are you? she'd asked.

No, I am not. Peter's heart ached with the memory as he looked into Jesus' face.

'Yes, Lord, you know I love you,' Peter replied. Silent tears dripped down his face now. Peter loved Jesus. He loved him more than life itself.

'Then take care of my sheep,' Jesus told him.

'Peter, do you love me?' Jesus asked a third time. Peter remembered his third denial, that he had denied even knowing who Jesus was. He remembered the rooster's crow and the heaviness it had brought.

Was this the reason that Jesus asked him three times? Were his questions giving Peter a second chance? Peter wiped the tears from his cheeks, sat up straight, looked into Jesus' eyes, and told him the truth, truth that came from the very core of his being.

'Lord, you know everything. You know I love you.' Peter searched Jesus' face once more. It was clear that Jesus' eyes saw more than just what was on the surface. Peter saw only love in his eyes. Jesus loved him, and Peter didn't deserve his love.

'Then feed my sheep,' Jesus told him.

Realisation swept over Peter. Jesus had given him a second chance to deny him or to choose him. He'd failed the first time, when asked three times that night around the fire, but when Jesus asked him three times now, around this fire, Peter was restored.

Jesus took away his guilt and bought Peter back into his fold with three simple questions. He loved Peter and Peter would do whatever he asked of him. He would look after Jesus' sheep, his followers, for all of his days.

A third time he asked him, 'Simon son of John, do you love me?'

Peter was hurt that Jesus asked the question a third time. He said, 'Lord, you know everything. You know that I love you.'

Jesus said, 'Then feed my sheep.' (John 21:17)

Birthday

Jesus walked by a group of people. They didn't recognise him, but he could overhear their conversation. They were talking about him.

'He can't be the Messiah,' a woman told her husband. 'Will the Messiah come from Galilee?'

'Well, the scriptures clearly state the Messiah will be born of the royal line of David,' her husband replied. 'He will be born in Bethlehem, the village where King David was born.'

Jesus recalled sitting in his family home, a warm, peaceful memory. He remembered the stories his parents would tell him of the day he was born, the cloth he was wrapped in, and the manger where they laid him. Of the journey his parents had taken, and the night they had searched for somewhere to rest in his birth town—the town of Bethlehem.

He smiled to himself.

Others said, 'He is the Messiah.' Still others said, 'But he can't be! Will the Messiah come from Galilee? For the Scriptures clearly state that the Messiah will be born of the royal line of David, in Bethlehem, the village where King David was born.' (John 7:41–42)

Talmo

Talmo sat with his friends. They were all there, but he sat between his favourites—Tide and Archie. They had met to speak about Jesus. Again. It was all they ever spoke about these days.

Talmo had a knot forming in his stomach. He wasn't concerned about Jesus' teachings or the way the people flocked to him. He wasn't concerned about how they would arrest him or when they should attack. No, Talmo wasn't concerned about any of the things his friends were meeting about … because Talmo had a secret. It was a secret he could never share and one he wished wasn't true. But every day, as Talmo met with his friends and listened to their evolving plans, his secret quietly gnawed away at him. It seemed to be becoming harder to sit through their meetings.

The secret he could never share was that Talmo believed in Jesus. For the life of him, he couldn't figure out why, but something had changed inside Talmo when he listened to Jesus speak. As a Jewish teacher, this was something Talmo could never ever admit to. So he sat silently in their meetings, umm-ing and ah-ing and nodding along with the others when appropriate. But for the most part, he remained quiet.

Today was no different. They were talking about the Passover celebration, about how they intended to have Jesus arrested and bought in for questioning. Talmo looked at his hands resting on the table before him.

'Is everything okay, Talmo?' Tide whispered. Talmo sat up straight in his chair. Tide knew him well. They had been close since childhood and Talmo had never kept a secret like this from Tide before. Talmo plastered on his most convincing smile.

'I'm good,' he whispered. Tide nodded but didn't look convinced. He turned his attention back to Beer, who led today's meeting.

'It is time to act,' Beer announced, hitting his hands on the table. Talmo jumped at the sound, and Tide looked at him again, concerned. Those around the table nodded in agreement, anticipation in the air.

'Can we get a show of hands?' Beer asked. It was something they did when a decision was to be made. They all realised it wasn't necessary on this occasion, as everybody obviously wanted Jesus stopped. But they raised their hands anyway, for the sake of tradition.

This was it. Talmo's palms grew clammy and his heart raced. Talmo had been able to remain quiet for the most part, uninvolved and unseen, but now he would need to raise his hand. They would notice if he did not.

All eyes followed the risen hands around the room until it was Talmo's turn. He paused for only a moment before raising his along with the others. But even as he raised it, the knot in his stomach turned and he was aware his raised hand went against everything his heart now believed in and everything his soul now knew to be true. His arm felt heavy as he held it in the air.

How had this happened? How had Talmo come to the conclusion—without even meaning to—that Jesus was the Messiah?

Many people did believe in him, however, including some
of the Jewish leaders. But they wouldn't admit it for fear
that the Pharisees would expel them from the synagogue.
For they loved human praise more than the praise of God.
(John 12:42–43)

Thank you that I don't have to pretend.

My heart has heard you say, 'Come and talk with me.'
And my heart responds, 'Lord, I am coming.'
(Psalm 27:8)

Raya

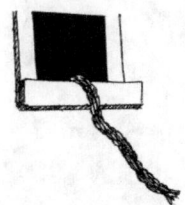

It had been a quiet, still voice, but a voice all the same. The two words played over and over again in Raya's mind.

Help them.

She had known the men were Israelites from the moment they'd arrived at her door. It wasn't just because of their lack of interest in her profession—Raya was a prostitute by trade—or even because of their accents. It had been something else. There was something about the Israelite men hiding on Raya's rooftop that she couldn't put her finger on. It was as though the men carried something with them that couldn't be seen. Although their nation was without a home, it was almost as though they had a reassurance. A reassurance that was steady and sure, and felt a lot like the words spoken into Raya's ear the moment she opened her door to them.

Help them.

Ordinarily, Raya would have called the authorities on the men. She knew why they were here. They had come to spy on the land. Everybody was talking about it and living in fear. The Israelites' God was all-powerful. He had moved mountains for his people, and it seemed he would give them Raya's homeland as their own. So Raya had decided to listen to the voice. She had taken the men to her rooftop, and just in time. When the authorities knocked looking for them, Raya lied. She told the officers the spies had indeed been here but had already left town.

Raya locked her front door and slowly let out her breath. She was acting against her better judgment. Raya climbed the steps up to her rooftop. The men were hidden beneath the bundles of flax she had laid out. They were dead silent.

'It's me,' Raya whispered. The men sighed with relief as they popped their heads out. 'They know you were here, but I told them you already left. They are searching for you now.'

The Israelites looked at each other, surprise on their faces.

'Thank you,' one of them finally said. 'May I ask why you are helping us?'

Raya sighed and sat down before them. She thought about telling them about the small voice, but decided against it.

'I know the Lord has given you this land,' she said. The men's eyes grew wide. They had clearly not expected her to say that.

'We are all afraid of you. We have heard how the Lord made a dry path for you through the Red Sea when you left Egypt. No one has the courage to fight after hearing such things. The Lord your God is the supreme God of the heavens above and the earth below.' Raya hadn't meant to say that last bit, but as the words streamed out, she felt the truth behind them.

The men remained silent, letting Raya speak, though it was clear they agreed with all that she said. Raya played with a scarlet rope lying at her feet, nervously twisting it between her fingers.

'I have to ask …' she faltered, then sat up straight, crossing her legs before her and holding the rope with both hands. She looked the men square in the eye. 'Because I have helped you today, would you be kind to me and my family when your God gives you this land?'

The men did not miss a beat.

213

'We will,' they replied, and relief washed over Raya. 'We offer our lives as a guarantee for your safety. If you don't betray us, we will keep our promise and be kind to you when the Lord gives us this land.'

Raya nodded as tears filled her eyes. The men came out from beneath the flax, and one took the scarlet rope from Raya's hands.

'You must leave this scarlet rope hanging from the window through which you let us down. And all your family members—your father, mother, brothers and all your relatives must be here inside the house.'

Raya took the rope from his outstretched hand and led the men to her window. It was dark outside now and Raya's home was built into the town wall. She let the men down by the scarlet rope. As they ran off into the distance, Raya tied the rope above her window so it was clear to see. She watched the rope beside her face as it swayed in the breeze. This rope that would save her life.

Then, since Rahab's house was built into the town wall, she let them down by a rope through the window.

'When we come into the land, you must leave this scarlet rope hanging from the window through which you let us down. And all your family members—your father, mother, brothers, and all your relatives—must be here inside the house. (Joshua 2:15, 18)

The Message

Isaiah knew there was real reason to fear and he understood why King Ahaz was afraid, but Isaiah knew better. He carried with him a message for King Ahaz. If heeded, the message could change everything.

Isaiah's son Shear walked beside him, their footsteps the only sound for miles.

'How will we find him?' Shear asked. Isaiah stopped and looked ahead.

'This way.' Isaiah pointed towards the aqueduct. Shear didn't question his father. Shear understood the source of Isaiah's wisdom, so he simply nodded.

King Ahaz was in serious trouble. His kingdom had been threatened by the kings of Syria and Israel. King Ahaz would have no chance of standing against their combined forces. Rumour had it that King Ahaz was terrified. It was said that his heart was trembling with fear, like a tree shaking in a storm.

Isaiah and Shear continued on to the end of the aqueduct that fed water into the upper pool. Isaiah knew this road well. It led to the field where cloth was washed. But this was the place. Isaiah stopped walking and Shear stopped beside him, looking to his father.

Both were quiet.

Isaiah slowly turned, scanning from where they stood until he spotted him in his hiding place. The king.

King Ahaz stood alone, in an alcove beside the wall. Even from where Isaiah stood, he sensed the great fear welling up inside the king. The fear reached his eyes, now darting from left to right.

Isaiah nodded at the king, and Ahaz stepped out from his hiding place beside the aqueduct. Shear kept his eyes to the ground as a sign of respect. He was supposed to be here, but Shear would remain silent from now on, present only as an observer.

'I have a message for you, Ahaz,' Isaiah said.

Ahaz listened. It was clear from the desperation in his eyes that he had lost all hope.

The sound of the water lapping beside them filled the empty space as Ahaz waited for Isaiah to continue.

'The Lord has said that I should tell you to stop worrying.' Isaiah paused, watching Ahaz's face as the words washed over him. 'You do not need to fear the fierce anger of those two burned-out embers, the kings of Syria and Israel.'

As Isaiah spoke, Ahaz's shoulders gave way, shaking and trembling, and he lost his composure. His eyes welled over, visibly giving way to the deep fear that had settled over his spirit. Ahaz knew he could trust Isaiah's words. Isaiah heard from the living God. Everyone knew this.

Isaiah continued. 'The Sovereign Lord says, "This invasion will never happen, it will never take place."' Isaiah went on to explain what the Lord would do, and how he would do it.

Ahaz took deep breaths, inhaling and exhaling, his faith rising as he listened. Suddenly Isaiah stopped speaking and looked Ahaz squarely in the eyes. Isaiah reached out a hand and held Ahaz's shoulder before delivering his final parting message.

'The Lord says, "Unless your faith is firm, I cannot make you stand firm."'

Ahaz stood tall beneath Isaiah's grip. He held his head high and a look of determination replaced the fear in his eyes as Ahaz remembered who he was and in whose protection he found refuge.

Then the Lord said to Isaiah, 'Take your son Shear-jashub and go out to meet King Ahaz. You will find him at the end of the aqueduct that feeds water into the upper pool, near the road leading to the field where cloth is washed. Tell him to stop worrying. Tell him he doesn't need to fear the fierce anger of those two burned-out embers, King Rezin of Syria and Pekah son of Remaliah.'

'This invasion will never happen; it will never take place … Unless your faith is firm, I cannot make you stand firm.'
(Isaiah 7:3–4, 7, 9)

Finger Drawing

She stood beside him, trembling with fear, and his heart went out to her. She had made a mistake. But instead of drawing her near, he dropped to the ground before her accusers, the men who wanted to see her stoned to death. She had committed adultery and had been caught. Jesus was aware that many of her accusers had committed adultery themselves—the only difference being that they had not been caught. Her accusers were teachers, and Jesus had heard them this very morning reading to the people from the book of Jeremiah.

> *Lord, you are the hope of Israel … those who turn away from you will be written in the dust because they have forsaken the Lord, the spring of living water.* (Jeremiah 17:13 NIV)

He took his forefinger to the dust around his sandals and he wrote down their names. He began with the oldest then continued on down the list until he had them all. Each and every one of her accusers, written in the dust.

Eco

For the life of him, Eco couldn't find his trumpet. He'd searched high and low all morning, and was becoming agitated. He wanted to make an offering in town, but couldn't do it without his trumpet. What would be the point?

Eco sat down on the seat in his living room and massaged his temples. Where could it be? Had he loaned it to someone who had forgotten to return it? Or had it been stolen from his home? He scowled.

Perhaps it was under his storage cupboard, out the back. He hadn't checked there. He jumped up and headed out back, and got down on his hands and knees. To his delight, the tip of his trumpet poked out from beneath the cupboard. Phew. His plans for the day were back on track. He would have had to postpone his offering if he'd been unable to find his trumpet.

Eco collected the offering he'd decided to give, placing the coins inside his bag. With his trumpet under one arm, he headed out the door. He would try to find a homeless person first. Eco didn't mind who it was, as long as the person was on a busy street, close to the centre of town.

It was a good time of the day. People would be out and about, attending to their business by now. It didn't take long for Eco to find somebody who looked hungry. She was a child, about ten years old. Most importantly, she stood on a crowded street. Perfect.

Eco stood for a moment, looking at those who were passing by, hoping to see someone he knew. It took a couple of minutes before he spotted a familiar face—Davi, who lived in Eco's neighbourhood. Davi was with some other men who Eco recognised. Good. Eco was sure they would recognise him too.

But Davi and the men were heading off down the street, so Eco would need to move fast. He took large strides across the road until he stood right beside the child. She looked at him with puffy eyes. Clearly, she'd been crying. Eco didn't pay her much attention. He was in a rush. He pulled his trumpet out from beneath his arm and blew into it. He'd had a lot of practice at playing the trumpet.

Eco blew as loud as he could, keeping his eyes on the men as they turned to see what was happening. Many others who were passing by stopped to watch, curious as to what Eco would do. Excellent! When Eco had enough attention, he put down his trumpet, fetched the coins from his bag and held them up as high as he could before the crowd. There were oohs and aahs, and a few people clapped for Eco. He nodded and tried to look as humble as he could. Eco handed the coins over to the starving child. He hoped those present would go home and tell their families about how generous he was.

'Watch out! Don't do your good deeds publicly, to be admired by others, for you will lose the reward from your Father in heaven. When you give to someone in need, don't do as the hypocrites do—blowing trumpets in the synagogues and streets to call attention to their acts of charity! I tell you

the truth, they have received all the reward they will ever get. Give your gifts in private, and your Father, who sees everything, will reward you. (Matthew 6:1–2, 4)

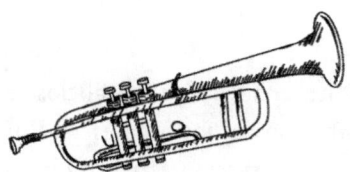

The Sycamore-fig Tree

The seed fell on the soil close to the road, closer to the road than any of the other trees. But it needed to be close.

The sycamore tree took root and began to grow. Over many years it grew, little by little, until it was both tall and strong. Then it waited for the day when it would become part of His story.

Being so close to the road, the tree was an easy option for those passing by. It was swung on, leaned on, and enjoyed by many.

There were conversations about cutting the tree down. After all, it was too close to the road. But it needed to be there, so it was protected.

The sycamore tree sensed in its branches that the time drew near. As its figs blossomed and grew, it stood tall and waited.

Then the morning arrived. A large crowd gathered on the road around the sycamore tree and a man climbed into the leafy branches. The man was too short to see over the crowd. He needed a tall tree, close to the road, that he could climb quickly. A tree so he could see Jesus.

As Jesus moved down the road, he headed for the sycamore tree, stopping before it and looking up into the branches.

'Zacchaeus!' he called to the man in the tree. 'Quick, come down! I must be a guest in your home today.'

The sycamore branch shook as Zacchaeus jumped from his perch and landed on the ground in front of Jesus.

So he ran ahead and climbed a sycamore-fig tree beside the road, for Jesus was going to pass that way. (Luke 19:4)

Tola

Tola was very wealthy, and had everything money could buy. But there was one thing Tola didn't have, one thing she had longed for—for many years. Tola didn't have a child. It had not been for lack of trying, but as the years went on and Jud, Tola's husband, became older, her hope of ever becoming a mother all but evaporated. Tola tried to count her blessings. She knew she had many. She had never been hungry or thirsty or without a place to live. She had fine clothing and a beautiful home. God had certainly blessed her. But other days were harder. Today, it seemed, was one of these.

Tola stood in the marketplace, her latest purchase under her arm, and watched the young children playing together around the well in the centre of town. They giggled and squealed as they ran into each other, tripping over themselves with excitement. It was moments like these, when Tola opened herself up to what might have been, that the lump in her throat made it hard to swallow. She blinked back her tears, readjusting the new blanket beneath her arm, and turned to head home. Sometimes she would stand there for far too long, but today she had a project so she would keep her mind busy.

Tola and her husband had extended their home, building a room on their rooftop, and Tola was having far too much fun decorating the new room. She had hung new curtains and painted the walls a soft yellow before adding a large, comfortable bed with a side table, a chair, and a lamp. Now

Tola held a warm blanket for the bed. If she was right, one of the colours in the blanket was close to the paint she had chosen for the walls.

Hopefully Elisha would visit their town again soon so he could see the room she had prepared for him. There had been something about Elisha from the moment she'd met him. Tola had watched him for some time before she'd felt compelled to invite him for dinner. She had wondered about him and felt drawn towards him, asking him question after question as they ate together. She'd invited him to stop in for a meal any time he was in town. Elisha had accepted her invitation and Tola had found herself looking forward to his next visit. She had been right about Elisha—there was something extraordinary about him. Tola had discussed it with Jud one evening.

'I am sure Elisha is a holy man of God,' she'd said. 'Let's build a small room for him on the roof and furnish it with a bed, a table, a chair, and a lamp. Then he will have a place to stay whenever he comes by.' Jud was happy for Tola to go ahead with her plans. He knew her well enough to know that once she had a brilliant idea, it was near impossible to stop her. So it wasn't long before work on the upper room was underway.

Tola spread the blanket out over Elisha's bed. She'd been right. The yellow paint matched perfectly.

As Tola prepared dinner that evening, she wondered about what Elisha's reaction might be. She hoped he would love the room as much as she did, and that he wouldn't think her odd for preparing it for him. She was tipping the potatoes from her pot onto the serving dish when she got the impression somebody was watching her. Tola glanced up. There was Elisha, standing in the doorway, his servant on the doorstep behind him.

'You're here!' Tola was delighted.

Elisha smiled in response. He was a quiet man, and Tola had grown to love his gentle ways.

'I need to show you something.' Tola clapped her hands together and placed her dishcloth on the table, excitement taking hold. She led Elisha and his servant out the door and up the stairs leading to the rooftop.

Tola opened the bedroom door and stepped inside, inviting Elisha to follow.

'We built this room for you. We hoped you would stay when you visit town.' She felt shy and hoped Elisha wouldn't feel they had overstepped their place.

Elisha didn't say much as he looked around the space, but Tola wondered if there was a shimmer in his eye.

'Thank you,' he finally whispered, looking deep into Tola's eyes. Too deep. Tola shifted uncomfortably.

'You are most welcome,' she replied, trying to sound cheerful and lighten the mood. 'Are you hungry?'

Throughout dinner, Tola felt Elisha's eyes on her. It seemed she had caught his attention and it made her nervous. Tola chatted about Jud's day at work and the weather and anything else she could think of.

Later in the evening, when Elisha had gone up to his room, his servant knocked on her door.

'Is everything okay?' Tola asked Elisha's servant.

'Yes, ma'am. Thank you.' He nodded. 'My master has asked me to tell you we appreciate the kind concern you have shown us.'

Tola grinned. She was so pleased to have blessed Elisha.

'He wants to know what we can do for you,' the servant said.

So that was what was going on. Elisha wanted to repay

Tola, to thank her. But there was no need. Tola needed nothing.

'Can we put a good word for you to the king or the commander of the army?' the servant asked. They were lovely ideas, but there was no need.

'No,' she replied. 'My family takes good care of me, but please thank Elisha for thinking of me.' The servant nodded and headed back up to Elisha's room.

Tola wiped down the table, thinking of Elisha up in the new bedroom, but her joy turned to sadness as her mind wandered back to the children she'd watched dancing around the well earlier in the day.

Jud had headed to bed for an early night. Maybe she should join him. She felt weepy and tired. She sighed to herself. Suddenly Elisha's servant was back in the doorway. Tola jumped a little, surprised to see him back so soon.

'Elisha would like to see you,' he announced.

'He would?' Tola straightened up, placed the dishcloth on the bench and followed his servant up to the bedroom.

Elisha was sitting on his bed. She was pleased to have him in her home and to see the new bedroom in use.

'Is everything okay?' she asked.

Elisha didn't reply. Instead, he looked Tola in the eyes. Minutes passed, and Tola shifted uncomfortably from one foot to the other until a quiet whisper settled over her soul and a peace she couldn't explain seemed to reach for her from within the bedroom, drawing her in and enveloping her.

Elisha finally spoke. 'Next year at this time, you will be holding a son in your arms.' Tola shook her head. What was he saying? What was he thinking?

'No, my lord!' she said. 'O man of God, don't deceive me and get my hopes up like that.' But even as she spoke the words, her hope rose. A shift inside her spirit, a knowing, that Elisha spoke the truth. Tears fell from her eyes as his words washed over her like waves.

You will hold a son. You will hold a son in your arms.

One day Elisha went to the town of Shunem. A wealthy woman lived there, and she urged him to come to her home for a meal. After that, whenever he passed that way, he would stop there for something to eat.

She said to her husband, 'I am sure this man who stops in from time to time is a holy man of God. Let's build a small room for him on the roof and furnish it with a bed, a table, a chair, and a lamp. Then he will have a place to stay whenever he comes by.'

Later Elisha asked Gehazi, 'What can we do for her?'

Gehazi replied, 'She doesn't have a son, and her husband is an old man.'

'Call her back again,' Elisha told him. When the woman returned, Elisha said to her as she stood in the doorway, 'Next year at this time you will be holding a son in your arms!'

But sure enough, the woman soon became pregnant. And at that time the following year she had a son, just as Eisha had said. (2 Kings 4:8–10, 14–16, 17)

Ask Him

John couldn't speak. He was shocked into silence, along with the other disciples sitting around the dinner table. It wasn't unusual—Jesus often said things that made John uncomfortable—but this was shocking. John looked around the table at his friends' faces, trying to imagine who it might be. Surely Jesus had it wrong this time. He must have it wrong. Although evidence of John's time spent with Jesus until now would suggest otherwise.

John stole a glance back to Jesus, who sat on the chair beside him. John knew Jesus well and could see he was troubled. The shallow lines beneath his eyes appeared deeper than usual.

I tell you the truth one of you will betray me. John replayed Jesus' words, his mind reeling.

The disciples murmured quietly among themselves, and John turned back to his meal. He knew they would be asking each other the same question, trying to figure out which of them would ever do such a thing. John's stomach turned, and he placed the piece of bread in his hand back on his plate. He was no longer hungry.

John felt somebody's eyes on him. He glanced up. Simon Peter sat directly across from him and looked at him intently. Did he have something to say? John raised his eyebrows at Simon, questioning.

'Who is he talking about?' Simon mouthed the words, motioning toward Jesus with his head.

John shrugged in response. He had no idea. Simon motioned again with his eyes toward Jesus. He wanted John to ask Jesus who would betray him. If anyone could ask, it was John. John nodded slightly at Simon, and then he looked at Jesus again. John tried to read his face, to gauge what his response might be.

Jesus was John's friend, and he didn't think he'd ever seen him so distressed. If only he could help him. He placed his hand on Jesus' shoulder, and Jesus turned toward him. John leaned in close. He paused for a moment.

'Lord, who is it?' he whispered so the others wouldn't hear.

Jesus looked at John for a minute, thoughtful. John loved the way Jesus looked at him. No one had ever loved John the way Jesus loved him. John knew Jesus trusted him. Every day John grew and changed, trying with all his might to be the man Jesus saw in him. But would Jesus tell him who the betrayer was? John wasn't sure.

'It is the one to whom I give the bread I dip in the bowl,' Jesus told him quietly.

John held his breath as he watched Jesus take a piece of bread from his plate, dip it into the bowl before them, and hand the bread across the table to Judas. John watched as Judas nodded, thanking Jesus. John watched as Judas took the bread straight to his mouth, and the noise of the room faded into the background as John watched Judas chew it.

John let out the breath he'd been holding. It was Judas.

Now Jesus was deeply troubled, and he exclaimed, 'I tell you the truth, one of you will betray me!' The disciples looked at each other, wondering whom he could mean. The disciple Jesus loved was sitting next to Jesus at the table. Simon Peter motioned to him to ask, 'Who's he talking about?' So that disciple leaned over to Jesus and asked, 'Lord, who is it?' (John 13:21–25)

Guilt

Pilate didn't usually come to the stone pavement this late at night. In fact, he had never sat alone on the platform like this before. It was an eerie feeling. He looked out at the courtyard where the crowds usually gathered, remembering back to earlier in the day when they had chanted for Jesus' life to be taken. Pilate couldn't understand why it had gotten beneath his skin, but it had and now he couldn't sleep.

His home stretched out before him to the left of the courtyard, and a candle burned in the windowsill of his wife's bedroom. She hadn't wanted Jesus to die. She had thought him innocent, and Pilate hadn't heard a word from her since his decision.

He sighed loudly to himself and looked up to the stars above. It was a starry night, and Pilate could breathe more easily out here. Perhaps he would stay out here all night. After all, he was probably being too hard on himself. Jesus was just one man, albeit an innocent man. Surely nothing much would result from Pilate's decision to have him killed.

When they said this, Pilate brought Jesus out to them again. Then Pilate sat down on the judgment seat on the platform that is called the Stone Pavement (in Hebrew, Gabbatha). (John 19:13)

Ari

Ari was excited to find the teacher. Mama told him they could pack a picnic and make a whole day of it. He'd seen the man once before, from a distance. Ari could remember his kind eyes.

He'd heard stories from the children of miracles they had seen. He was excited, anticipating what might happen today.

Ari and Mama set off down the road. It wasn't long before they were joined by others in search of the teacher.

The crowd grew until there were so many people Ari had to hold on tight to Mama's hand.

Dust flew everywhere from the many feet hitting the dirt road. It wasn't long before a rumour spread through the crowd. The teacher had been spotted on a hill beside the Sea of Galilee.

Ari skipped with excitement, one hand clutching his lunch pouch and the other firmly holding his mama's.

When they arrived at the hill, Ari saw the teacher. He was seated on the grass with some other men.

Ari pried himself loose from his mother's grip and bolted towards them.

He stopped before reaching the group. The teacher's back was towards him, but Ari could see his brown hair and his hands resting on his knees. Maybe he could walk around the group to get a closer look at the teacher's face.

One of the men noticed Ari. The man walked toward him. Ari looked back at the crowd, for Mama. She waved and Ari was reassured that she was watching.

'Hi, there,' the man said.

'Hello,' Ari replied.

'Are you on your own?' The man knelt face-to-face with Ari.

'No. Mama's on her way.' Ari puffed. 'I ran because I want to sit up close.'

'Good idea, by the look of that crowd!'

'My Mama said we could stay all day.' Ari liked the man.

'Did she now?' He raised his eyebrows.

'Yes, she made us a picnic.' Ari opened his lunch pouch and revealed its contents.

'Andrew!' one of the men called. The man jumped to his feet and returned to his friends.

The hours flew by on the hilltop. When the teacher spoke, the crowd was quiet like nothing Ari had seen. Children were made to keep quiet in the temple, but they'd never been this quiet.

The sea breeze blew against Ari's face and he played with the grass at his fingertips.

In the afternoon, the teacher and his disciples took a break, chatting among themselves. Ari watched Jesus push the hair back from his face and smile when he was spoken to. He wasn't in a rush like Ari's father often was.

Andrew, who had spoken with Ari earlier, caught his eye. Andrew beckoned for him to join them. Ari looked up at his mother, who nodded her permission.

Ari stepped up to the group and sat beside Andrew and listened to the men's conversation.

'Where can we buy bread to feed all these people?' Jesus

asked. Ari watched his face. Jesus didn't seem worried, but the man he spoke to looked worried. Ari recognised the look on his face. He looked like the way Ari felt when Mama asked him to clean up.

'Even if we worked for months, we wouldn't have enough food to feed them,' the man told Jesus. He was right. Ari looked out at the ocean of people.

'There's a boy here with five barley loaves and two fish.' Andrew pointed at Ari.

'But what good is that with this huge crowd?'

That was the moment. Jesus looked at Ari for the first time. Ari felt a stirring in his belly. It wasn't just hunger, but something about the way Jesus looked at him.

He beckoned for Ari to come. Ari jumped to his feet and kept his eyes on Jesus.

Jesus looked from Ari to the lunch pouch in his hand. Ari quickly held it up, offering it to the teacher.

Jesus opened Ari's pouch.

'Tell everyone to sit down,' he said.

The people were seated and a hush fell over the crowd.

There was a sea of faces looking toward Jesus. Ari stood beside Jesus as he cleared his throat and looked towards heaven.

Jesus thanked God for Ari's barley loaves. Ari watched as Jesus broke the bread and handed it to his disciples, who handed it to the people.

Ari knew there wouldn't be enough. What would Jesus do when the food was gone? But each time the loaves were dispersed, Jesus reached into Ari's lunch pouch and pulled out another.

When all the people had loaves, Jesus took Ari's fish. He thanked God for it, and distributed it to the people.

Ari stood beside Jesus, looking out at the thousands of people. They were eating and talking.

But how? Ari felt Jesus place his hand on top of his head. He knelt beside Ari.

'Thanks for sharing your lunch, Ari.'

Ari thought his chest might explode as he wrapped his arms around Jesus' neck.

He clutched his pouch and ran through the crowd to find his mother.

Tears were streaming down her face when Ari plonked down beside her. He didn't understand. She smiled as she pulled Ari close. He decided she wasn't sad and opened his lunch pouch. It was full of barley loaves and fish.

Jesus soon saw a huge crowd of people coming to look for him. Turning to Philip, he asked, 'Where can we buy bread to feed all these people?' He was testing Philip, for he already knew what he was going to do.

Philip replied, 'Even if we worked for months, we wouldn't have enough money to feed them!'

Then Andrew, Simon Peter's brother, spoke up. 'There's a young boy here with five barley loaves and two fish. But what good is that with this huge crowd?' (John 6:5–9)

You come close again.
The barrier between us was man-made.

I see that the Lord is always with me.
I will not be shaken, for he is right beside me.
No wonder my heart is glad,
and my tongue shouts his praises!
My body rests in hope.
Acts 2:25–26

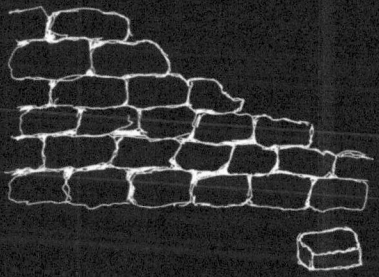

March Thirty-first

It had been thirty-seven years, and King Jehoia was tired. He had lost all hope. It felt like a lifetime since the day of his great fall. King Jehoia's kingdom and his homeland had been destroyed, exiled to Babylon. Jehoia's life hung by a thread.

Jehoia stunk, and his prison gown was revolting. He lived in filth, the likes of which he had never known. Jehoia's own mother, Nehushta, had died beside him, here in prison. Some days, Jehoia yearned for the end of his life too.

God had forgotten Jehoia and his people—Jehoia was sure of that. There had been a time when Jehoia and his people were named God's 'own special possession'. They were set apart, precious to God. But that time had come to an abrupt end.

Jehoia, along with his people, had betrayed God. He could see that now. Their punishment was great, and Jehoia had become sorry as the years passed by. They had been unfaithful to the God of the universe. They had worshipped other gods, gods they themselves had created. Jehoia had had a lot of time to think on these things—thirty-seven years! He had realised that his people had pierced God's own heart. That their betrayal had hurt the living God. That their loyalty meant something to him. Jehoia hadn't realised. He hadn't understood.

Rumour had it amongst the prison guards that Evil-merodach had ascended to the Babylonian throne. Jehoia listened as discreetly as he could when the guards spoke beside the prison door. This news was not good for Jehoia. It was dangerous to be in prison when one king was succeeded by another. Lives hung in the balance.

He didn't sleep well that night. He was used to the concrete, but nightmares of the new king dragging him from his cell and torturing him in unspeakable ways had him tossing and turning through the hours of darkness. It was early the next morning before Jehoia finally slept. Then he was woken by the sound of the prison gate screeching open beside where he lay. Jehoia sat straight up. He knew better than to continue resting when the guards entered the cells. His vision was blurry and his mind was playing catch-up, but he did his best to look alert.

There were two guards this morning. Jehoia was careful not to look them in the face.

'You.' One guard pointed his finger at Jehoia. 'Come with us.'

This was it. Jehoia swallowed over the lump in his throat as he obeyed the guard. He stood, steadying himself with one hand on the wall. He kept his eyes to the ground and followed the men. What would they do to him? How would he die today? The blood rushed from his head, and it took all his concentration to stay upright. He followed the set of feet before him, leaving the iron gates behind.

He prayed. 'God, if you still hear me… God, if you are here in this place with me, please help me now.' It was a simple prayer, all Jehoia had. His eyes filled with tears as he stepped one foot after the other down long, isolated corridors and then out into an open space. The sun pouring through a window shocked him—it had been many years. Jehoia was overwhelmed and about to die.

Jehoia was brought before Evil-merodach. He stood alone, dirty, humiliated, and humbled. He had once stood in Evil-merodach's shoes, and now here he was. Jehoia waited for the king to speak, to hear his fate.

'King Jehoia of Judah?' Evil-merodach said.

'Yes,' Jehoia replied.

'The days of your captivity have come to an end.'

Because the day of his death had arrived? Jehoia waited silently, holding his breath, all too aware of the armed guards who stood at either side of the king.

'Look at me,' Evil-merodach said.

Jehoia was surprised but obeyed the king. He looked from the floor up into the king's eyes, and what he saw shocked him. Evil-merodach looked at him with kindness.

'What I mean is …' King Evil-merodach cleared his throat. 'Today, on the thirty-first of March, your captivity ends. You will no longer live in the prison cell. You will be given new clothing to replace your rags, and you will eat with me, here in the palace.'

Was he joking? Jehoia was speechless. His mouth gaped but no words came out, and his trembling hands clenched together as the king's words wrapped around him.

Would Jehoia live to see another day after all? Was Evil-merodach really bringing his days of captivity to an end?

And was the God of the universe not so far from Jehoia after all?

In the thirty-seventh year of the exile of King Jehoiachin of Judah, Evil-merodach ascended to the Babylonian throne. He was kind to Jehoiachin and released him from prison on March 31 of that year. (Jeremiah 52:31)

Eye Witness

John watched as the soldiers broke the legs of the prisoner who hung on the cross beside Jesus. He wanted to look away, to yell, and to scream out. He wanted to be sick, but instead he winced and watched to see what they would do to Jesus. The soldiers stood beneath Jesus' cross with their heads stretched back, looking up at him.

'He's dead,' John heard one of them say.

'That was fast,' the other replied.

John held his breath and relief rushed over him as he saw the soldiers step away from Jesus' body. They wouldn't break his legs because he was already dead. John drew in another deep breath and held it as he watched Jesus' face hanging low. Tears dripped from John's chin. Jesus was dead. He was really dead.

One of the soldiers turned back towards Jesus, and John watched in anguish as the soldier took his spear and pierced it into Jesus' side. A cry escaped John's lips as both water and blood gushed out of the wound. John wrung his fingers together. They had pierced him, and he was really gone.

But when they came to Jesus, they saw that he was already dead, so they didn't break his legs. One of the soldiers, however, pierced his side with a spear, and immediately blood and water flowed out. (This report is from an eye-

witness giving an accurate account. He speaks the truth so that you also may continue to believe.) These things happened in fulfilment of the Scriptures that say, 'Not one of his bones will be broken,' and 'They will look on the one they pierced.' (John 19:33–37)

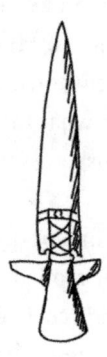

His Love

She stood on white marble floors that glistened beneath her bare feet. Was this real? It felt like a dream ... but it was not. She looked down at her hands, turning them over. They were younger than she remembered, the skin tighter than it had been.

She looked up to his judgment seat and her eyes slowly rose until they met with his. She gasped. Instantly, she dropped to her knees before him, the weight of him filling her veins, filling her body from the bottom of her feet right up to the top of her head. Electricity shot through her body, and the skin on her palms tingled. Her lips felt on fire and her ears burned with heat. She didn't need to ask him her question because she could already tell.

She could see it in his eyes. He loved her.

Remember, we will all stand before the judgment seat of God. For the Scriptures say, "'As surely as I live,'" says the Lord, "every knee will bend to me, and every tongue will confess and give praise to God.'" (Romans 14:10–11)

Released

'He is ours,' the voices of death chimed. Excitement took hold, for the Son of God had died and he was now surrounded by darkness. He was finally theirs. Jesus sat in the darkness, his legs folded beneath him.

Death watched on, waiting for Jesus' light to go out. But Jesus' light did not go out. Death frowned. This hadn't happened before. Death watched him, suspicious. Any time now, his light would become dark. It had to.

But it did not. Jesus was quiet and still, waiting.

Three days and three nights went by. Although surrounded by death, surrounded by darkness, his light remained, shining bright. Death screamed with frustration. Desperate, Death tried to touch Jesus with his darkness but was repelled by the warmth of Jesus' light.

What was this? It seemed that Death had no power over him. But that was impossible. For everything that was dead belonged to Death.

As Death looked on, his impatience bubbling over, the unthinkable happened. From deep within the light that surrounded him ... Jesus took a breath.

Mary was standing outside the tomb crying, and as she wept, she stooped and looked in.

'Mary!' Jesus said. She turned to him and cried out, 'Rabboni!' (which is Hebrew for 'Teacher').

'Don't cling to me,' Jesus said, 'for I haven't yet ascended to the Father. But go find my brothers and tell them, 'I am ascending to my Father and your Father, to my God and your God.' (John 20:11, 16–17)

But God released him from the horrors of death and raised him back to life, for death could not keep him in its grip. (Acts 2:24)

Thank you for reading my stories through to the end. I hope you heard him whisper to you through the lines and the pages, and I hope you remembered that he sees you and knows your story.

That he listens to your words as you string together sentences and he watches your life with love-shaped eyes.

That when the cross weighed him down and he struggled to keep moving, he took another step because he thought of you.

He thought of your family, of your bloodline, of that beautiful familiarity you get when you step into your home and close the door to the world behind you.

Of your life.

He thought of you.

– Stacey

www.ingramcontent.com/pod-product-compliance
Lightning Source LLC
Chambersburg PA
CBHW070558120726
47909CB00007B/2376